PENGUIN CLASSICS

THE EXETER BOOK RIDDLES

Kevin Crossley-Holland was educated at Bryanston School and St Edmund Hall, Oxford. He was Gregory Fellow in Poetry at the University of Leeds from 1969 to 1971 and Lecturer in Anglo-Saxon Literature and Culture for the Tufts-in-London Program from its inception in 1967 until 1978. He now holds the Endowed Chair in the Humanities and Fine Arts at the University of St Thomas in Minnesota. His *New and Selected Poems* were published in 1991 and he is the translator and editor of *The Anglo-Saxon World* (1982). His versions of *The Norse Myths* were published by Penguin in 1982 and among his books for children are *Beowulf* (1982), *Storm*, awarded the Carnegie Medal for 1985, *British Folk Tales* (1987) and *Tales from Europe* (1991). Kevin Crossley-Holland has collaborated with a number of composers, including Nicola LeFanu, with whom he wrote the opera *The Green Children*, and Sir Arthur Bliss and William Mathias, both of whom set to music some of the riddles in this book.

THE
EXETER BOOK
RIDDLES

TRANSLATED AND INTRODUCED BY
KEVIN CROSSLEY-HOLLAND
Revised edition

PENGUIN BOOKS

PENGUIN BOOKS

Published by the Penguin Group
Penguin Books Ltd, 27 Wrights Lane, London w8 5 tz, England
Penguin Books USA Inc., 375 Hudson Street, New York, New York 10014, USA
Penguin Books Australia Ltd, Ringwood, Victoria, Australia
Penguin Books Canada Ltd, 10 Alcorn Avenue, Toronto, Ontario, Canada m4v 3 b2
Penguin Books (NZ) Ltd, 182–190 Wairau Road, Auckland 10, New Zealand

Penguin Books Ltd, Registered Offices: Harmondsworth, Middlesex, England

This collection first published as *The Exeter Riddle Book* by
the Folio Society 1978
Published in Penguin Classics 1979
Revised edition 1993
1 3 5 7 9 10 8 6 4 2

Riddles 29, 30a, 47, 57, 77, 81 and 85
are reprinted by kind permission of
Novello & Co. Ltd

Typeset by Datix International Limited, Bungay, Suffolk
Set in Monotype Garamond
Printed in England by Clays Ltd, St Ives plc

CONTENTS

FOREWORD TO THE REVISED EDITION

As more than thirty years have elapsed since I began to translate the Anglo-Saxon riddles, I decided to give my translations a spit-and-polish before putting them on parade again. On closer inspection, though, I found many of my lines approximate or inelegant – the work of a wilful apprentice and of a stranger. So I have spent this wolf-winter with the riddles on my desk, and sat side by side with the scribe whose travail Riddle 51 movingly portrays:

> Dreag unstille
> winnende wiga se him wegas tæcneþ
> ofer fæted gold feower eallum.

In this second edition, only a dozen of my original translations survive intact. I have revised the remaining sixty-three, some lightly, some so heavily that the revisions offered here are effectively retranslations.

KEVIN CROSSLEY-HOLLAND
Northfield, Minnesota

INTRODUCTION

The nature of the riddle

The business of naming began with the Creation; the business of deceiving followed soon after, in the Garden of Eden. It is reasonable to suppose that as soon as men had wits they delighted in riddling. And they have delighted in it ever since: metaphor and simile, the detective story, the faked voice on the telephone, the crossword puzzle, the question in the cracker – they all hinge on recognition and, because they represent things as other than they are, they are all living members of the riddle family.

It was Aristotle who first put his finger on the similarity between riddle and metaphor. In his *Rhetoric*, he wrote:

While metaphor is a very frequent instrument of clever sayings, another or an additional instrument is deception, as people are more clearly conscious of having learned something from their sense of surprise at the way in which the sentence ends and their soul seems to say, 'Quite true and I had missed the point.' This, too, is the result of pleasure afforded by clever riddles; they are instructive and meta-phorical in their expression.

Just so, and many of Aristotle's fellow countrymen are reputed to have lost their lives for being unable to answer the semi-metaphorical riddle: 'What has one voice, and goes on four legs in the morning, two legs in the afternoon, and three legs in the evening?' This is, of course, the famous enigma that the Sphinx, that fabulous winged beast with the head of a woman and the body of a lion, put to each passer-by as she sat by the precipice outside Thebes. Those who were unable to answer she either devoured or hurled over the edge. And when Oedipus volunteered, 'It is man, who goes on all fours as a baby, who walks upright in the prime of his life, and who hobbles with a stick in old age,' the enraged Sphinx threw herself over the precipice.

We know that Egyptians, as well as Greeks, liked riddling, and there are riddles in the first sacred book of the Brahmans, the *Rig Veda*. One of them depicts the year as a twelve-spoked wheel upon which stand 720 sons of one birth (the days and nights); and a comparable riddle turns up in an early Persian collection which describes knights (the days of the month) riding before the Emperor. These Time-Riddles are one of a number of universal riddle motifs – which is why they are also called 'World-Riddles' – and find their counterpart in the twenty-second riddle of the *Exeter Book*, 'The Month of December'. There are riddles in the Koran, too, and in the Bible there is, *inter alia*, the impossibly difficult riddle that Samson asked the Philistines at Timnah: 'Out of the eater came forth meat, and out of the strong came forth sweetness.' Delilah seduced Samson into telling her the answer (a honeycomb in the carcass of a dead lion) and paid Samson out by passing it on to the Philistines.

The word 'riddle' derives from the Old English *rædan*, to advise, to counsel, to guide, to explain. And in a wide sense a riddle does teach: it presents the old in new ways. To men sitting at the mead-bench, listening to the professional poet or taking the harp and themselves improvising, the riddle redefined the familiar. The Anglo-Saxon cast of mind and literary mode seems ideally suited to the metaphorical riddle when one considers that the entire body of Old English poetry is packed out with mini-riddles; they are known as 'kennings', and are in fact condensed metaphors. The sea is described as 'the swan's riding-place', 'the ship's road' and 'the whale's path'; a sail is spoken of as 'a sea-garment', a poet as 'a laughter-smith' and a wife as 'a peace-weaver'. Setting aside puns and conundrums and catch-questions, of which there are only a handful in the *Exeter Book*, what is a riddle but an extended kenning?

The Exeter Book

The first bishop of Exeter was Leofric. He died in 1072 and amongst his bequeathals to the Cathedral Library was *.i. mycel englisc boc be gehwilcum pingum on leoðwisan geworht*, 'one large book in English verse about various subjects'. This has always been taken to be the *Codex Exoniensis* or *Exeter Book*, one of the four great surviving miscellanies of Old English poetry. Probably copied by one scribe during the last quarter of the tenth century, this manuscript consists of 131 leaves or folios and contains a great range of poetry. There are 'documentary' Christian poems, such as 'Christ', which relates the Nativity and the Ascension and anticipates the Day of Judgement; there are Christian allegories about 'The Panther' and 'The Whale', which turn up again in many medieval bestiaries, and 'The Phoenix' (a godsend of a bird because of its supposed miraculous resurrection); there are elegiac poems, such as 'The Wanderer' and 'The Seafarer' (memorably translated by Ezra Pound), that are ostensibly Christian in their comparison of the transient life on earth with the eternal life in heaven, but which celebrate the old Germanic qualities of endurance and resilience, tempered by melancholy; there are poems such as 'Widsith' and 'Deor' that draw on the traditions and stories of the pagan Germanic world, survivals of the time before the Angles, Saxons, Frisians and Jutes first came to England; and, of course, there are the riddles. The *Exeter Book* is a remarkable anthology and, had it not survived, we would have to suppose the range of Old English poetry to be much narrower than we know it to be.

That the manuscript has survived seems virtually accidental. It is possible to deduce from gaps in the text that at least seven folios are missing. At some time it appears to have been used both as a cutting-board, perhaps a sort of bread-and-cheese board, and as a beer-mat; there are scores and circular stains on the first folio. More seriously, the manuscript has also been damaged by fire. A long diagonal burn on the last fourteen folios has destroyed the text of some of the later riddles, the last group of which are the final entry in the manuscript.

The number, condition, authorship, date of composition and sources of the riddles

There are ninety-six riddles in the *Exeter Book* and they have been copied into the manuscript in three groups: Riddles 1–59, Riddles 30b and 60, and Riddles 61–95. Because one folio is missing between Riddles 40 and 41 (see Notes to those riddles) it is generally thought that, as with other earlier collections in Latin, there were originally one hundred riddles. It is the third group that has suffered because of the burn in the manuscript.

There is not, and is not likely to be, academic agreement over the authorship of the *Exeter Book* riddles. For a long time the eighth-century poet, Cynewulf, was believed to have composed them all. Now, conversely, most commentators suppose that the collection is the work of many hands, and that Cynewulf's was not one of them. In the words of Krapp and Dobbie, editors of *The Anglo-Saxon Poetic Records*, 'The question may, therefore, hardly be said to be definitely settled; but the burden of proof seems to be upon those who would demonstrate unity of authorship.' The date of composition is similarly uncertain, and all the more so because of the likelihood of multiple authorship, although there is linguistic evidence that a handful of the riddles were composed in the first half of the eighth century. In this context, Krapp and Dobbie write: 'It is of course very likely that a large number of the riddles date from the early eighth century, when Englishmen were most active in the composition of Latin riddles, but a more definite statement than this is hardly possible in the light of our present knowledge.'

Who were these English riddlers writing in Latin, and what bearing do they have on the *Exeter Book* collection? The first question is easy to answer, the second less so. There are three surviving collections in Latin. They are ascribed to Aldhelm (*c.* 640–709), who was Abbot of Malmesbury and subsequently Bishop of Sherborne, and who wrote one hundred riddles or *Ænigmata*; to Tatwine (d. 734), who was an Archbishop of Canterbury; and to Eusebius (*c.* 680–*c.* 747), who is believed to be one and the same as Hwætberht, Abbot of Wearmouth and a friend of Bede. The riddles by Tatwine and Eusebius are preserved in the same manuscript and together number one hundred – Tatwine was responsible for forty and Eusebius sixty. Aldhelm acknowledges as his model Symphosius, whose collection of one hundred riddles also survives, and who is credited with originating the literary riddle in post-Classical times. He is thought to have lived in the late fourth or early fifth century.

Much valuable work has been done recently on the sources and analogues of the riddles, and it is clear that the three collections by Englishmen and the earlier collection by Symphosius were all known to the *Exeter Book* riddlers. In one or two cases, for example Riddle 40 (see Notes), the Anglo-Saxon riddler attempted a translation and elaboration of the Latin original; in several instances the correspondence between Old English and Latin is very close; while in a number of other cases either the Anglo-Saxon riddler borrowed and very freely developed an idea in one of the Latin riddles, or else both

Anglo-Saxon and Latin riddles are analogues, referring to the same traditional material. In so far as possible, the Notes to the riddles identify any known Latin source or analogue.

It should not be supposed, though, that the *Exeter Book* riddles are a collection of half-baked derivations. On the contrary they have great imaginative zest, great charm, and at times great subtlety; they are wonderfully attractive in their own right.

The elements of the collection

In many ways the riddles constitute a delightful and inform-ative entrée into the Anglo-Saxon world. Some are folk-riddles (distinguished by their use of popular material, their shortness and simplicity), some are literary riddles (full of conscious poetic elaboration and attention to detail), and some combine both elements. Just as the tone and treatment varies from one riddle to the next, so does the subject-matter itself. As one turns from natural phenomena to animal and bird life, from the Christian concept of the Creation to humdrum domestic objects, from weaponry to the peaceful pursuits of writing and music, one wins glimpse after glimpse of the Anglo-Saxons and their attitudes.

It may be worth looking at the elements of the collection in a little more detail. Typically enough, more than a dozen riddles are concerned with weapons and war-gear and contest – sword, for instance, and shield, bow, battering ram. This is what one would expect of a society caught up in almost endless turmoil – against the Romano-British, against each other, against the Vikings and, finally, against the Normans. It was a society whose values had changed very little despite migration from the European Continent, the advent of Christi-anity and the passage of time. Describing the way of life of the German tribes living within the Roman Empire in the first century, Tacitus noted in his *Germania*: 'As for leaving a battle alive after your chief has fallen, that means lifelong infamy and shame. To defend and protect him, to put down one's own acts of heroism to his credit – that is what they really mean by allegiance. The chiefs fight for victory, the companions for their chief.' And again: 'A man is bound to take up the feuds as well as the friendships of father or kinsman.' The bond between chief and followers, the emphasis on kinship, on physical and moral courage and on the blood-feud were just as important to the Anglo-Saxons at the Battle of Hastings as to their Germanic ancestors in the first century. These are the tremendous words of Byrhtwold at the end of 'The Battle of Maldon' (991) after his lord had been slain and the Danes, the war-wolves, are on the brink of victory:

> Harder heads and hearts more keen,
> spirits on fire as our strength flags!
> Here lies our leader, axed and limp,
> the top dog in the dust. He who turns
> from this war-play now will mourn
> for ever. I am old. I'll stay put.
> I'll lay my pillow on the ground
> beside my dear man, my loved lord.

The deserter was condemned to live an unenviable life of exile, and the fundamental lord–retainer relationship is touched on in several of the riddles. So too is the overriding sense of *wyrd* – fate – and the need to struggle against it, which dogged the pagan tribes that first came to England and their descendants, the Anglo-Saxons. This was a society whose greatest ambition was for fame despite all; the last word of *Beowulf* describes that hero as *lofgeornost*, 'most eager for fame'. One of the Old Norse sayings attributed to Odin very nicely sums up the pagan Anglo-Saxon's attitude to life: 'One thing I know never dies or changes, the reputation of a dead man.'

Just as some riddles in the *Exeter Book* reflect aspects of the Germanic heroic world, others describe objects, such as the Bible and chalice, associated with the new Christian faith that swept through England during the seventh century. One can visualize what hope Christian teaching must have brought, the hope of a life after death. Nothing exemplifies it quite as well as the much-quoted words of one of King Edwin's councillors (related by Bede), when that King was considering whether or not to adopt the new Christian faith:

O King, imagine you are sitting at a banquet with your ealdormen and thanes in winter time; the fire is burning and the hall is warm, and outside the winter storms are raging; and there should come a sparrow flying swiftly through the hall, coming in through one door and out by another. While it is inside, it is safe from the winter storms; but after a few minutes of comfort, it soon returns from winter back to winter again, and is lost to sight. Likewise, this mortal life seems like a short interval; what may have come before, or what may come after it, we do not know. Therefore, O King, if this new Christian teaching brings any great certainty, it seems fitting that we should follow it.

King Edwin followed it!

During the seventh and eighth centuries, the scriptoria of the great Northumbrian monasteries produced a steady stream of manuscripts (see Note to Riddle 26), for use at home and for missionary activity on the Continent. There are several riddles about the work of the scribe, the illumination of manuscripts, and the custody of books – including a charming short poem about a bookmoth – while another group of riddles is concerned with musical instruments that would have been heard inside and outside the monastery: harp, horn, reed-flute and bagpipe.

Although the *Exeter Book* riddles reflect aspects of Germanic heroism and of Christianity, in either case quite formal and dignified, the foremost preoccupation of the collection is with the everyday life of working people, with household objects, and with aspects of the natural world. There are riddles about bucket and bellows, churn and key, ale and mead, anchor and plough; riddles about badger and bullock, the swan, the jay, the swallow, the copulating cock and hen; riddles about the sun and moon, and sudden storms, and ice. They are informed by sharp observation, charm, an earthy sense of humour, above all by a sense of wonder – and they make us in turn recognize that every object around us has its distinctive attributes and a life of its own. Even if the riddlers were clerics (as they doubtless were) the majority of the riddles reflect the views of people who may have been aware of fate and of God, and struggled manfully to reconcile the two, but were in the end more concerned with crops than concepts. The Anglo-Saxons were above all an agricultural people and, more than any other literature that survives from the period, this riddle collection is the song of the unsung labourer.

In surveying the constituents of the *Exeter Book* collection, it only remains to mention the six runic riddles. 'Rune' means 'mystery' or 'secret' and the runic alphabet is thought to have originated at the beginning of the Christian era. It consisted of twenty-four letters (known as the *futhark*) and each letter had its name and meaning: the letter D, for instance, is represented by ⋈ in the runic alphabet, and its name was *dæg*, 'day'. Since the letters consist entirely of vertical and diagonal strokes, and use no curves or horizontals, it is thought likely that the alphabet was originally designed for use on wood and metal. It was first used for magical purposes but was used more generally in Anglo-Saxon England, sometimes for protective purposes (runes engraved on a sword blade, for example), and sometimes for identification. The *Exeter Book* riddlers used runes instead of, or as well as, poetic ambiguity – a kind of additional conundrum.

It is with these runic riddles, and with the punning Riddle

30a, that the *Exeter Book* collection comes closest to the catch-question riddle that has doubtless prospered in every age, and that most children have up their sleeves today – the riddle more concerned with the value of words than with the object described. This kind of riddle must have reached its apogee with the Victorians: Why is a good meerschaum like a water-colour artist? *Because it draws and colours beautifully*. Why has the Dark Continent no terrors for Mr Stanley? *Because he 'makes light' of it*. What part of a fish is like the end of a book? *Don't you know? Why, the fin-is*. Teasers of this kind can be fun and they can be extremely boring. But either way they are devoid of poetry. The glory of the *Exeter Book* collection is that it consists of riddles which are, at their best, excellent enigmas *and* excellent poems.

Principles of translation and arrangement of the volume

All Old English poetry, and about 30,000 lines survive, was composed in stately, pounding four-stress lines, with at least two of the stresses (one of them invariably the third) emphasized by alliteration. The vocabulary of the poet was formal; it made use of many compounds and of the kennings to which I have already alluded. The language of the poet, no less highly wrought than the work of the jeweller, must have seemed to the Anglo-Saxons just as artificial as Spenser's language did to Elizabethan ears. The difference is that Anglo-Saxon poets were working within an oral tradition.

In translating these riddles, I have settled for a non-syllabic four-stress line, controlled by light alliteration. My diction inclines to the formal – although it is by no means as highly wrought as that of the original poets. I have understood my first duty as a translator (as opposed to an imitator) to be to convey the actual meaning of the Anglo-Saxon, and have with respect tried to follow the example set by Alfred, who

wrote in his Preface to Gregory's *Pastoral Care* that he trans-
lated *hwilum worde be worde, hwilum andgit of andgiete*, 'Sometimes
word for word, sometimes sense for sense'. But I have also
pursued the elusive spirit of the originals, and if some of the
translations are also thought to read as poems in their own
right, so much the better.

In this volume, the main text includes translations of
seventy-five of the ninety-six *Exeter Book* riddles – all those
that are not either very badly damaged or impossibly obscure.
The original numbering of the riddles has been adopted, and
this means that the main text has a broken sequence of num-
bers. The Notes at the end of the book deal with all the
riddles consecutively and include translations of sixteen of the
remaining riddles. No translations are offered for the remain-
ing five riddles for reasons stated in the notes on them.

Acknowledgements

I have translated from the text of the standard edition of *The
Exeter Book* (*Anglo-Saxon Poetic Records III*), edited by George
Philip Krapp and Elliot van Kirk Dobbie (New York, 1936).
In discussing possible solutions, it will be evident that I have
made use of the meticulous summaries prepared by Krapp
and Dobbie, and have also taken particular account of the
opinions expressed in *The Riddles of the Exeter Book*, edited by
Frederick Tupper (Boston, 1910), *Old English Riddles*, edited
by A. J. Wyatt (Boston, 1912), and *Anglo-Saxon Riddles of the
Exeter Book*, translated by Paull F. Baum (Durham, North
Carolina, 1963). When I have provided a solution to a riddle
without equivocation, it means that all commentators have
agreed upon it. I must also acknowledge my extensive use of
Sources and Analogues of Old English Poetry, translated by Michael
J. B. Allen and Daniel G. Calder (Cambridge, 1976).

Some of the riddles in this volume were first published in

my translations of *The Battle of Maldon and Other Old English Poems* (London, 1965) and *Storm and Other Old English Riddles* (London, 1970), and I have made some use both of the latter and of my introduction to the Anglo-Saxons, *Green Blades Rising* (London, 1974), in preparing this Introduction and the Notes.

I began to translate the Old English riddles shortly before coming down from Oxford in 1962. This book therefore celebrates a fifteen-year involvement, and I cannot fully acknowledge the stimulus and assistance so many people have given me over that period. There are, though, some friends whom I must thank now in public and particular. Bruce Mitchell, my tutor and then my collaborator, first excited and unobtrusively guided my adult interest in the Anglo-Saxons and their literature, and he offered me line-by-line criticism of the translations of many of these riddles; George MacBeth gave me a BBC platform for the first group of riddles I translated; and Sir Arthur Bliss provided a great stimulus by setting some of them to music. I have discussed the translations and possible solutions with many friends, and owe a special debt to Marni Hodgkin for helping to shape *Storm and Other Old English Riddles* and to Richard Barber for his most helpful critical suggestions over a number of years. Val Kwaan offered valuable criticism of the Introduction; Rosamond Richardson has given me generous support and encouragement when it mattered; and lastly I sincerely thank John Letts, whose idea it was that I should translate the *Exeter Book* riddles entire.

THE RIDDLES

I

Who is so clever and quick-witted
as to guess who goads me on my journey
when I get up, angry, at times awesome;
when I roar loudly and rampage over the land,
sometimes causing havoc; when I burn houses
and ransack palaces? Smoke rises,
ashen over roofs. There is a din on earth,
men die sudden deaths when I shake the forest,
the flourishing trees, and fell timber –
I with my roof of water, an avenger
driven far and wide by the powers above;
I carry on my back what once covered
every man, body and soul submerged
together in the water. Say what conceals me
or what I, who bear this burden, am called.

2

Sometimes I plunge through the press of waves,
surprising men, delving to the earth,
the ocean bed. The waters ferment,
sea-horses foaming . . .
The whale-mere roars, fiercely rages,
waves beat upon the shore; stones
and sand, seaweed and saltspray, are flung
against the dunes when, wrestling
far beneath the waves, I disturb the earth,
the vast depths of the sea. Nor can I escape
my ocean bed before he permits me who is my pilot
on every journey. Tell me, wise man:
who separates me from the sea's embrace,
when the waters become quiet once more,
the waves calm which before had covered me?

3

Sometimes my Lord corners me;
then He imprisons all that I am
under fertile fields – He frustrates me,
condemns me in my might to darkness,
casts me into a cave where my warden, earth,
sits on my back. I cannot break out
of that dungeon, but I shake halls
and houses; the gabled homes of men
tremble and totter; walls quake,
then overhang. Air floats above earth,
and the face of the ocean seems still
until I burst out from my cramped cell
at my Lord's bidding, He who in anger
buried me before, so shackled me that I
could not escape my Guardian, my Guide.

Sometimes I swoop to whip up waves, rouse
the water, drive the flint-grey rollers
to the shore. Spuming crests crash
against the cliff, dark precipice looming
over deep water; a second tide,
a sombre flood, follows the first;
together they fret against the sheer face,
the rocky coast. Then the ship is filled
with the yells of sailors; the cliffs quietly
abide the ocean's froth and fury,
lashing waves, racing rollers
that smash against stone. The ship must face
a savage battle, a bitter struggle,

if the sea so buffets it and its cargo
of souls that it is no longer under control
but, fighting for life, rides foaming
on the spines of breakers. There men see
the terror I must obey when I bluster
on my way. Who shall restrain it?

At times I rush through the dark clouds
that ride me, churn the sea into a frenzy,
then afterwards let the water subside.
When one cloud collides with another,
edge against sharp edge, the din
of destruction, a mighty noise, echoes
above the dwellings of men; dark bodies,
hastening, breathe fire overhead,
flashing lightning; thunderous crashes
shake the sky, then growl darkly.
The clouds do combat, dark drops
fall, rustling rain from their wombs.
A fear-tide flows in the hearts of men,
a growing terror – strongholds succumb
to dread – when that ghastly troop goes
on the rampage, and shrithing evil spirits,
spurting flames, shoot sharp weapons.
A fool is unafraid of the death-spears,
but for all that he will die
if the true Lord lets fly the arrow,
a whistling weapon, straight through rain
from the whirlwind above. Few men
survive if they are struck by lightning.
I am the origin of all that strife,
when I rush through the concourse of clouds,
surge forward with great strength, and fly
over the face of the water. Troops on high

clash noisily; then, afterwards,
under cover of night, I sink to earth,
and carry off some burden on my back,
renewed once more by my Lord's power.
I am a mighty servant: sometimes
I fight, sometimes wait under the earth;
at times I swoop and sink under water,
at times whip up waves from above;
sometimes I rise, stir up trouble
amongst scudding clouds; swift and savage,
I travel widely. Tell me my name,
and Who it is rouses me from my rest,
or Who restrains me when I remain silent.

4

Ring me, they ring me. I work long hours
and must readily obey my master,
break my rest, and loudly proclaim
that my guardian gave me a halter.
A man or a woman, weary and bleary,
has often called on me; winter-cold
I answer them, surly as they are. Sometimes
a warm limb looses the bound ring.
But it delights my master, a dull sort
of man, and satisfies me into the bargain,
if anyone can fathom and solve my riddle.

5

I'm by nature solitary, scarred by iron
and wounded by sword, weary of battle.
I often see the face of war, and fight
hateful enemies; yet I hold no hope
of help being brought to me in battle
before I'm cut to pieces and perish.
At the city wall sharp-edged swords,
skilfully forged in the flame by smiths,
bite deeply into me. I must await
a more fearsome encounter; it is not for me
to find a physician on the battlefield,
one of those men who heals wounds with herbs.
My sword wounds gape wide and wider;
death blows are dealt me by day and by night.

6

Christ, the true giver of victories,
created me for combat. When my lord
urges me to fight, I often scorch mortals;
I approach the earth and, without a touch,
afflict a huge host of people.
At times I gladden the minds of men,
keeping my distance I console those
whom I fought before; they feel my kindness
as they once felt my fire when,
after such suffering, I soothe their lives.

7

Silent is my dress when I step across the earth,
reside in my house, or ruffle the waters.
Sometimes my adornments and this high windy air
lift me over the livings of men,
the power of the clouds carries me far
over all people. My white pinions
resound very loudly, ring with a melody,
sing out clearly, when I sleep not on
the soil or settle on grey waters – a travelling spirit.

8

I've one mouth but many voices;
I dissemble and often change my tune;
I declaim my deathless melodies
and don't refrain from my refrain.
Aged evening-songster, I entertain
men in their homes by rehearsing
my whole repertoire; they sit, bowed down,
quiet in their houses. Guess my name,
I who mimic the jester's japes
as loudly as I can, and rejoice men
with choicest songs in various voices.

9

In former days my mother and father
forsook me for dead, for the fullness of life
was not yet within me. But a kinswoman
graciously fitted me out in soft garments,
as kind to me as to her own children,
tended and took me under her wing;
until under shelter, unlike her kin,
I matured as a mighty bird (as was my fate).
My guardian then fed me until I could fly
and wander more widely on my
excursions; she had the less of her own
sons and daughters by what she did thus.

10

My beak was bound and I was immersed,
the current swept round me as I lay covered
by mountain streams; I matured in the sea,
above the milling waves, my body
locked to a stray, floating spar.
When, in black garments, I left wave
and wood, I was full of life;
some of my clothing was white
when the tides of air lifted me,
the wind from the wave, then carried me far
over the seal's bath. Say what I am called.

I I

My garb is ashen and in my garments
bright jewels, garnet-coloured, gleam.
I mislead muddlers, despatch the thoughtless
on fool's errands, and thwart cautious men
on their useful journeys. I can't think
why, addled and led astray, robbed
of their senses, men praise my ways
to everyone. Woe betide addicts
when they bring the dearest of hoards on high
unless they've foregone their foolish habits.

1 2

I travel by foot, trample the ground,
the green fields, for as long as I live.
Lifeless, I fetter dark Welshmen,
sometimes their betters too. At times
I give a warrior liquor from within me,
at times a stately bride steps on me;
sometimes a slave-girl, raven-haired,
brought far from Wales, cradles and presses me –
some stupid, sozzled maidservant fills me
with water on dark nights, warms me
by the gleaming fire; on my breast
she places a wanton hand and writhes about,
then sweeps me against her dark declivity.
What am I called who, alive, lay waste
the land and, dead, serve humankind?

13

I saw ten in all, roaming the greensward,
six brothers strutting with their sisters;
they had living spirits. A garment of skin –
there was no mistaking it – hung on the wall
of each one's house. And none were worse off,
nor their movements more painful, though
they must gnaw at the grey-green shoots,
robbed of their garments, roused by the might
of the guardian of heaven. New clothing
is furnished for those who before walked out
naked; they scatter and roam over the land.

14

I was once a warrior's weapon.
Now a noble young retainer
dresses me in threads of twisted gold
and silver. At times men kiss me,
at times I summon close friends
to do battle; a horse sometimes bears me
over the earth, sea-horses sometimes
sweep me, gleaming, over the ocean;
now and then a maiden, ring-adorned,
replenishes my paunch. I must lie on planks
at times, plundered, hard and headless;
often, gold-garbed, I hang on the wall
above drinking warriors, a splendid sight,
instrument of war. Covered in riches,
I draw in breath from a brave man's lungs
when retainers ride towards battle.
At times I tell proud warriors
that wine is served; at times rally them,
save booty from hostile men, drive off
the enemy. Now ask me my name.

15

Whereas my neck is white, my head
and sides are brown; I move swiftly
and bear a battle-weapon; hair covers my back
and my cheeks as well; two ears tower high
above my eyes. I step on my toes through
the green grass. Grief is ordained for me
if any fierce creature should catch me
in my hole where I have my house and children;
should I stay there with my offspring
after this guest comes knocking
at my door, they are doomed to die.
I must bravely carry my infants
far from our house, and save them by flight,
if that creature still follows me.
He advances on his breast. I dare not await him
in my hole . . . that were not a wise plan at all.
I must burrow through the steep hillside
with my two forefeet as fast as I can.
I can save the lives of my loved ones
with ease, once I've guided them out
by a secret way through a hole in the hill.
Then, if it comes to blows and battle,
I feel no fear of this murderous foe.
If he still gives me chase
through that narrow hole I've just made in the hill,
I will not fail to fight him fiercely.
Once I've tunnelled my way to the top,
I will angrily batter my enemy,
that hateful foe from whom I long fled.

16

I must fight with the waves whipped up by the wind,
grapple alone with their force combined,
when I dive to earth under the sea.
My own country is unknown to me.
If I can stay still, I'm strong in the fray;
If not, their might is greater than mine,
they'll break me in fragments and put me to flight,
meaning to wreck what I must protect.
I can foil them if my fins are not frail,
and the rocks hold firm against my force.
You know my nature, now guess my name.

17

Confined by a wire fence, and filled
with princely treasures, I'm the bulwark
of my people. Many is the morning
I spew spear-terror; the more I'm fed,
the greater my strength. My guardian watches
how darts whistle out of my belly.
At times I almost swallow the burnished
dark bolts, the baleful weapons,
searing poisoned spears, esteemed by warriors.
Men remember what issues from my mouth.

20

I'm a strange creature, shaped for a scrap,
dear to my lord, finely decorated.
My clothing is motley and bright metal threads
mount the deadly jewel my master
gave me – the man who at times involves me
in a fight. I carry treasure then,
the handiwork of smiths, gold in the court,
all the clear day. I often despatch
well-armed warriors. A king enriches me
with silver and precious stones, honours me
in the hall; he doesn't stint but sings my praises
to the gathering – men swigging mead;
at times he holds me in reserve, at times
sets me free, travel-weary, eager
in the fray. Often I put friend
at the throats of friends; I'm widely reviled,
the most accursed of weapons. If a cruel warrior
should assault me in battle, I cannot hope
for a son to avenge me on my slayer;
nor will the family from which I sprang
be increased through children of mine
unless, lordless, I have to leave
the guardian who once gave me rings.
If I follow a warrior and fight on his behalf,
as I've done before for my master's satisfaction,
I must forego, as fate wills, the chance
to father children. I cannot lie
with a woman, but the same man who once
bound me with a belt denies me now

the rapture of loveplay; I must enjoy
the treasure of heroes single and celibate.
Tricked out with metal threads, I often
irritate and frustrate some woman; she insults me,
smacks her hands and runs me down,
yells abuses. This is not my kind of contest . . .

21

I keep my snout to the ground; I burrow
deep into the earth, and churn it as I go,
guided by the grey foe of the forest
and by my lord, my stooping owner
who steps behind me; he drives me
over the field, supports and pushes me,
broadcasts in my wake. Brought from the wood,
borne on a waggon, then skilfully bound,
I travel onward; I have many scars.
There's green on one flank wherever I go,
on the other my tracks – black, unmistakable.
A sharp weapon, rammed through my spine,
hangs beneath me; another, on my head,
firm and pointing forward, falls on one side
so I can tear the earth with my teeth
if my lord, behind me, serves me rightly.

22

Sixty men in company came
riding down to the estuary. Eleven
of those mounted men had horses
of peace, and four had pale grey horses.
The warriors could not cross the water
as they wished for the channel was too deep,
the shelf too abrupt, the current too strong,
the choppy waves thronging. Then the men
and their horses climbed on to a waggon – a burden
under the cross-bar; and then a single horse
hauled those proud spear-warriors with their steeds,
dragged the waggon right across the estuary,
although no ox, nor carthorse, nor muscular men
dragged it with him; and he did not swim,
nor wade because of his guests' weight,
nor muddy the water, nor ride on the wind,
nor double back. Rather, he carried
the warriors and their horses across the creek
from the steep bank, the staithe, so that they
stepped up bravely on the opposite side,
men and their mounts unscathed by water.

Wob is my name, if you work it out;
I'm a fair creature fashioned for battle.
When I bend, and shoot a deadly shaft
from my stomach, I'm very eager
to send that evil as far away as I can.
When my lord (he thought up this torment)
releases my limbs, I become longer
and, bent upon slaughter, spit out
that deadly poison I swallowed before.
No man's parted easily from the object
I describe; if what flies from my stomach
strikes him, he pays for its poison
with his strength — speedy atonement for his life.
I'll serve no master when unstrung, only when
I'm cunningly notched. Now guess my name.

24

I'm a strange creature with various voices:
I can bark like a dog, bleat like a goat,
honk like a goose, shriek like a hawk,
at times I mimic the ashen eagle,
the battle-bird's cry; the vulture's croak
trips off my tongue, and the mew of the seagull,
as I sit here, saucily. G suggests
my name, and Æ, R and O assist it,
so do H and I. I'm called
what these six characters clearly spell out.

25

I'm a strange creature, for I satisfy women,
a service to the neighbours! No one suffers
at my hands except for my slayer.
I grow very tall, erect in a bed,
I'm hairy underneath. From time to time
a good-looking girl, the doughty daughter
of some churl dares to hold me,
grips my russet skin, robs me of my head
and puts me in the pantry. At once that girl
with plaited hair who has confined me
remembers our meeting. Her eye moistens.

26

An enemy ended my life, took away
my bodily strength; then he dipped me
in water and drew me out again,
and put me in the sun where I soon shed
all my hair. The knife's sharp edge
bit into me once my blemishes had been scraped away;
fingers folded me and the bird's feather
often moved across my brown surface,
sprinkling useful drops; it swallowed the wood-dye
(part of the stream) and again travelled over me,
leaving black tracks. Then a man bound me,
he stretched skin over me and adorned me
with gold; thus I am enriched by the wondrous work
of smiths, wound about with shining metal.
Now my clasp and my red dye
and these glorious adornments bring fame far and wide
to the Protector of Men, and not to the pains of hell.
If the sons of men would make use of me
they would be safer and more sure of victory,
their hearts would be bolder, their minds more at ease,
their thoughts wiser; they would have more friends,
companions and kinsmen (true and honourable,
brave and kind) who would gladly increase
their honour and prosperity, and heap
benefits upon them, holding them fast
in love's embraces. Ask what I am called,
of such use to men. My name is famous,
of service to men and sacred in itself.

Favoured by men, I am found far and wide,
taken from woods and the heights of the town,
from the downs and the dales. During each day
corbiculas carried me through the bright sky,
with care they brought me to a safe shelter.
Then men bathed me in a tub. Now I bind
and chasten them, at once throw a young man
to the ground, sometimes an old churl too.
He who struggles against my strength,
he who grapples with me, will find
he must hit the hard floor with his back
unless he forgoes such a foolish fight.
Robbed of his strength, but not of his tongue,
he has no say over his mind
or his hands or his feet. Who knocks
young men stupid, and as his slaves binds them
in broad, waking daylight? Yes, ask me my name.

28

Some acres of this middle-earth
are adorned with the hardest and the sharpest,
most bitter of man's fine belongings;
it is cut, threshed, couched, kilned,
mashed, strained, sparged, yeasted,
covered, racked, and carried far
to the doors of men. A quickening delight
lies in this treasure, lingers and lasts
for men who, from experience, indulge
their inclinations and don't rail against them;
and then, after death, it begins to gab,
to gossip recklessly. Even clever people
must think carefully what this creature is.

29

I saw a strange creature,
a bright ship of the air subtly adorned,
bearing away plunder between her horns,
fetching it home from a foray.
She wanted to build a bower in the stronghold,
construct it with cunning if she could do so.
Then a mighty creature appeared over the mountain
– his face is known to all dwellers on earth;
he seized the treasure and sent home the wanderer
against her will; she went westward,
vowing revenge, hastening forth.
Dust lifted to heaven; dew fell on the earth,
night fled hence; and no one knew
thereafter, where that creature went.

30a

I'm surrounded by flames and sport with the wind,
I'm clothed in finery and the storm's great friend,
ready to travel, but troubled by fire,
a glade in full bloom and a burning flame;
friends often pass me from hand to hand,
and I'm kissed by ladies and courteous men.
When I raise myself, many people
bow before me; I bring
their happiness to full maturity.

31

This world is adorned in diverse ways,
decorated with rare ornaments.
I saw a strange thing singing in a house;
nothing on earth looked in the least
like this creature, her shape was so odd.
Her beak pointed upwards, her feet
and talons were those of a bird,
yet she cannot fly nor even move much,
though eager to start she sets to work
with her singular skills; often and again
she goes the rounds at gatherings of men,
she sits at the feast and awaits her turn –
it comes soon – to prove her prowess
in the halls of thanes. But there this creature
never partakes of what makes men merry.
Daring, eager for fame, she stays dumb;
and yet in her foot she has a fine voice,
the glorious gift of song. It is so
strange that this creature makes sense only
with her dangling foot, richly decorated.
When she holds her hoard, proud of her rings
yet naked, she bears her brothers on her neck –
a mighty kinswoman. Even a canny poet
will be hard put to name this creature.

32

This world is adorned in diverse ways,
decorated with rare ornaments.
I saw a strange contraption, a fine traveller,
grind against the grit and move, screaming.
The strange creature couldn't see; it had
no shoulders, arms or hands; this oddity
has to move on one foot, travel fast
over the salt-fields. It had many ribs,
and a mouth in its middle, useful to men.
It carries food in plenty, performs a service,
each year it yields men a gift used
by rich and poor. Tell me if you can,
O man of wise words, what this creature is.

33

A strange creature came floating over the waves,
she cried her beauty from ship to shore,
resounded loudly; her laughter was terrible
and fearsome to all; her edges were sharp.
She was so fierce – slow to engage,
savage in the fight; she stove in ships' sides.
She bound them with a baleful charm,
and spoke with native cunning:
'My mother, one of the beloved maidens,
is my daughter also, swollen and strong,
known by all people as she falls on the earth,
she stands in joy in every land.'

34

In the town I saw a creature
which feeds the cattle. It has many teeth;
its beak is useful as it points down,
gently plunders and turns for home;
it searches for plants along the slopes,
and always finds those not rooted firmly;
it leaves the living ones held by their roots,
quietly standing where they spring from the soil,
brightly gleaming, blowing and growing.

35

The dank earth, wondrously cold,
first delivered me from her womb.
I know in my mind I wasn't made
from wool, skilfully fashioned with skeins.
Neither warp nor weft wind about me,
no thread thrums for me in the thrashing loom,
nor does a shuttle rattle for me,
nor does the weaver's rod bang and beat me.
Worms that decorate the yellow web
never spun for me with the skills of the Fates.
Yet all over the earth one man will tell
another that I'm an excellent garment.
O wise man, weigh your words
well, and say what this object is.

37

I saw the creature: his stomach stuck out behind him,
enormously swollen. A strong servant
waited upon him. What filled up his stomach
had travelled from far, and flew through his eye.
He does not always die in giving life
to others, but new strength revives
in the pit of his stomach; he breathes again.
He fathers a son; he's his own father.

38

I saw a creature: masculine, greedy
with all youth's abandon. As his due
his guardian gave him four springs,
four fountains, shooting and shining.
A man spoke, he said to me:
'Alive, that creature breaks the downs;
dead and shredded, he binds the living.'

39

Books say this creature exists
amongst mankind, openly seen
as the seasons turn. It has a special power
far greater than people perceive. Its desire
is to seek out every living thing,
one by one; then it goes on its way.
It never spends two nights in the same place
but, homeless, follows forever the paths
of exile; no one despises it because of that.
It has neither hand nor foot, and never leaves
an imprint on the earth; no eyes either,
and no mouth, nor does it speak to men;
and it has no brain. But books explain
that this is the swiftest creature
ever conceived, of any species.
It lacks soul or life but must roam
far and wide through this wondrous world.
It lacks blood and bone yet benefits
many men throughout this middle-world.
It has never thrust to heaven, and never to hell,
but must exist always as the laws
of God decree. It would take long to tell
of how its life spins on, follows
fate's twisted pattern; that is a history
of marvels. Each and every word
describing this creature is true;
it has no offspring, it lives even so.
If you can answer quickly
and correctly, say what I am called.

Enduring the Creator, He who now guides
this earth on its foundations and governs this world.
Powerful is the Ruler, and rightly King
and Sovereign over all; He governs and guides
earth and heaven, and they are encompassed by Him.
He made me – a marvel – at the beginning,
when He first fashioned this circle of earth;
He ordained that I should stay awake
and never sleep again, and sleep suddenly
overtakes me, my eyes quickly close.
With His power the mighty Creator rules
this middle-earth in every respect;
so that I, at my Lord's leave,
embrace this circle of earth entire.
I'm so timid that a drifting ghost
can frighten me terribly, and from end
to end I'm bolder than a wild boar
when, bristling with fury, it stands at bay;
no warrior on earth can overcome me,
but only God, who governs and guides
this high heaven. My fragrance
is much fairer than frankincense or rose
        . . . grows in the greensward,
a delight; but I'm the more delicate;
although men love the lily of the field,
with its shining flower, I'm the finer;
so too with my sweetness, always and everywhere,
I overpower the aroma of spikenard,
and I'm more foul than this murky fen

that, festering here, reeks of filth.
I govern one and all under the circle
of heaven for, at the beginning, the beloved
Father enjoined me to be just
to thick and thin; I assume everywhere
the form and feature of each thing.
I'm higher than heaven and the High King
bids me behold His secret nature;
I also see everything under the world,
the dismal pits of depraved spirits.
I am much older than this circle of earth
or this middle-world could ever be,
and I was born yesterday – a baby
from my mother's womb, acclaimed by men.
I'm fairer than gold ornaments,
even if filigree work adorns them;
I'm more foul than this mouldering timber
or this slob of seaweed spewed up here.
I'm broader than the earth entire,
and more wide than this green world;
a hand can enclose me, and all that I am
can easily be held between three fingers.
I'm harsher and more biting than sharp frost,
the fierce rime that settles on the soil;
I'm hotter than the fire, the flames
surging and flickering at Vulcan's forge.
I am, besides, sweeter to the palate
than the honeycomb mingled with honey;
I'm more bitter than wormwood, too,
that stands, ashen, on this hillside.
I can gorge more greedily than an old giant,
holding my own in an eating match,
and I can always live content
if I see no food for as long as I live.

I can fly faster than the pernex,
the hawk or the eagle could ever do;
no Zephyr – that restless wind – ranges
as I do, rifling through every quarter;
the snail is swifter than I, the earthworm
more spry, and the fen frog outstrips me;
the son of dung (we call him
a weevil) crawls about more quickly.
I weigh much more than a grey boulder
or a hunk of lead, I'm much lighter
than this little insect that skitters
over the surface of the water with dry feet.
I'm tougher than flint, that strikes these sparks
from this adamant scrap of steel,
I'm much softer than this down, that here
in the wind wafts high into the air.
I'm broader than the earth entire
and more wide than this green world;
wondrously made with miraculous skill,
I embrace everything – and quite easily!
There's no creature below me
in this wondrous world; I'm exalted
above every one of our Lord's creations,
Who alone, with His eternal might, can forcefully
stop me from swelling up. I'm more massive
and mighty than the huge whale who peers
dimly at the ocean bed, stronger than he
and yet I've less muscle than a mere tick
which sensible men dig out with a knife.
No white locks, delicately curled, cover
my head, but I'm bald all over;
nor do I have eyelids or lashes,
they were all cut off by the Creator;
now, lovely to see, curled locks

spring from my scalp, and grow until they
shine on my shoulders – an utter marvel.
I'm greater and more gross than the fattened pig,
the grunting hog, who lives happily
in the beech-wood, muddy and rooting,
so that he . . .

42

I watched a couple of curious creatures
copulating openly, out of doors;
the fair-haired, flushed woman
got her fill under her garments
if the work was fruitful. I can tell men
in the hall – those who are well-versed – the names
of these creatures with runes. There shall be
Need (N) twice over, and one gleaming
Ash (Æ) on the line, two oaks (A)
and two Hailstones (H) also. With the key's power,
who has unlocked the treasury's chained door
that, firm in intent, denies runemen
access to the riddle, covered in its heart
with cunning bonds? Now they're exposed
to men drinking in the hall – the proper
names of this feather-brained pair.

43

I've heard tell of a noble guest;
man entertains him. He's not prey
to hunger pangs or burning thirst;
age and illness are unknown to him.
If the servant tends him well, satisfies
this guest who must go on a journey,
both will be happy in their home,
live in prosperity, surrounded
by a family; but there'll be sorrow
if the servant neglects his lordly guest,
his ruler on the journey. Think of them
as brothers, fearless of each other.
When they depart, together desert
one kinswoman (their mother and sister),
both suffer hurt. Let him who can
put names to the pair I describe —
the guest, then his servant, the host.

44

A strange thing hangs by a man's thigh,
hidden by a garment. It has a hole
in its head. It is stiff and strong
and its firm bearing reaps a reward.
When the man hitches his clothing high
above his knee, he wants the head
of that hanging thing to poke the old hole
(of fitting length) it has often filled before.

45

I'm told a certain something grows
in its pouch, swells and stands up,
lifts its covering. A proud bride grasped
that boneless wonder, the daughter of a king
covered that swollen thing with clothing.

46

A man sat sozzled with his two wives,
his two sons and his two daughters,
darling sisters, and with their two sons,
favoured firstborn; the father of that fine
pair was in there too, and so were
an uncle and a nephew. Five people
in all sat under that same roof.

47

A moth devoured words. When I heard
of that wonder it struck me as a strange event
that a worm should swallow the song of some man,
a thief gorge in the darkness on fine phrases
and their firm foundation. The thievish stranger
was not a whit the wiser for swallowing words.

48

I heard a radiant ring, with no tongue,
intercede for men, though it spoke
without argument or strident words.
The silent treasure said in front of men:
'Save me, helper of souls.'
May men understand the mysterious saying
of the red gold and, as the ring said,
wisely entrust their salvation to God.

49

I know something that stands earthfast;
deaf and dumb, in the daylight hours
it often devours useful gifts handed to it
by a servant. At times, in the houses of men,
some dark-skinned, swarthy slave
puts more into its mouth, dearer than gold,
things such as athelings, kings and queens,
dream of. But I will not name it,
this dumb creature here, this sombre nitwit,
that for their use gives back to brave men
exactly what it has eaten, earlier.

50

On earth there's a warrior of wondrous origin.
He's created, gleaming, by two dumb creatures
for the benefit of men. Foe bears him against foe
to inflict harm. A woman often fetters him,
strong as he is. If women and men
provide for him in the proper manner
and often feed him, he'll obey them
and serve them well. Those who succour him
win themselves pleasure. But this warrior savages
the man who lets him become proud.

5 1

I watched four curious creatures
travelling together; their tracks were swart,
each imprint very black. The birds' support
moved swiftly; it flew in the air,
dived under the wave. The toiling warrior
worked without pause, pointing the paths
to all four over the beaten gold.

52

I saw a couple of violent captives
carried in under the roof of the hall;
they were companions, tightly bound,
fettered together. Close to one
stood a dark-haired Welshwoman,
a slave to oversee the prisoners' movements.

53

I saw a tree with splendid branches,
towering in the wood; the timber grew,
a joyous growth. Both water and earth
fed him well, but when he grew old
his whole life became a misery;
sorely wounded, and silent in his chains,
his front was fettered with sombre trappings.
Now with brute force his butting-head
opens up the way for his owner,
a vile enemy. Often in the storm
have they plundered the treasure hoard together.
The man was swift and tireless if the first,
his comrade, was cornered and in danger.

54

A young man made for the corner where he knew
she was standing; this strapping youth
had come some way – with his own hands
he whipped up her dress, and under her girdle
(as she stood there) thrust something stiff,
worked his will; they both shook.
This fellow quickened: one moment he was
forceful, a first-rate servant, so strenuous
that the next he was knocked up, quite
blown by his exertion. Beneath the girdle
a thing began to grow that upstanding men
often think of, tenderly, and acquire.

55

I saw in the hall (where visitors were drinking)
a wondrous tree, of four timbers, brought
on to the floor; it was adorned with twisted gold,
plated with silver, inlaid with jewels
most skilfully, a symbol of His cross who for us
established a ladder between Heaven and Earth
before He harrowed Hell. I can easily
tell you of this tree's origin:
the hard yew and shining holly,
the maple and the oak serve their Lord
together and together share one name –
an outlaw's tree it was that frequently offered
a weapon to its lord, a treasure in the hall,
the gold-hilted sword. Now tell me the answer
to this riddle, whoever will hazard
a guess as to what this tree is called.

56

I was in a room where I watched a piece
of wood, a shuttling beam, scathe
a struggling creature; it sustained battle-wounds,
savage gashes. Spears were the bane
of this creature, and with skill the beam
had been fixed securely. One of its feet
stood firm, and the other strived busily,
pumped up and down, scraped the ground.
A tree stood nearby hung with bright
leaves. When spears had done their work,
I saw the leavings brought before my lord,
carried across the floor where warriors caroused.

57

This air bears little creatures
high over the hill-slopes. Black! they are black,
dressed in dark clothing. They travel in flocks,
singing loudly, liberal with their songs.
Their haunts are wooded cliffs, yet they sometimes
come to the houses of men. They name themselves.

58

I know a creature in the field with one foot
and derring-do. It does not range widely
or ride very far, nor can it fly
through the bright air, or embark on some ship
with nailed sides; nonetheless
it obliges its master on many occasions.
It has a heavy tail and a little head,
a long tongue but not one tooth;
part of it is iron; it passes through a hole
in the earth. It eats nothing, drinks no water,
frets for no fodder, and yet often carries
liquid aloft. It boasts neither life
nor gifts from a lord, but still obeys
its owner. Three fitting runes
form its name: R*ad* is the first.

59

I watched men, wise in their minds,
and in their hearts serene, gaze at a golden
ring in the hall. God the saviour
has prayed for peace abounding for each guest
who turns the ring; then that ring spoke
a word to the family, it named the guardian
of men who do good. Dumb as it was,
it clearly raised the image of the Maker
before the minds and eyes of anyone able
to understand the meaning of the gold
and the wounds of the Lord, and do as the wounds
of the ring ordained. If a man is unbaptised,
neither his prayer nor his spirit
can enter the kingdom of God,
the castle of heaven. Let him who will
explain how the wounds of this wondrous ring
spoke to men when it was turned in the hall
and passed through proud retainers' hands.

60

I sank roots first of all, stood
near the shore, close by the dyke
and dash of waves; few men
saw my home in that wilderness,
but each dawn, each dusk,
the tawny waves surged and swirled
around me. Little did I think
that I, mouthless, should ever sing
to men sitting at the mead-bench,
varying my pitch. It is rather puzzling,
a miracle to men ignorant of such arts,
how a knife's point and a right hand
(mind and implement moving as one)
could cut and carve me – so that I
can send you a message without fear,
and no one else can overhear
or noise abroad the words we share.

61

A lovely woman, a lady, often locked me
in a chest; at times she took me out
with her fingers, and gave me to her lord
and loyal master, just as he asked.
Then he poked his head inside me,
pushed it up until it fitted tightly.
I, adorned, was bound to be filled
with something rough if the loyal lord
could keep it up. Guess what I mean.

62

I'm strong and pointed. Shuddering I die,
a violent release. For my reputable master
I'll plunge below the plimsoll line,
well and truly engineer an opening.
A desperate man stands behind me and develops me
himself; he carries a cloth. A southerner sometimes
helps me out of a hot spot (a real hole),
sometimes he gets me into a fix
and forces me. Say what I am called.

65

Quick; quite mum; I die notwithstanding.
I lived once, I live again. Everybody
lifts me, grips me, and chops off my head,
bites my bare body, violates me.
I don't bite a man unless he bites me;
there are many men who bite me.

66

I stretch beyond the bounds of the world,
I'm smaller than a worm, clearer than the moon,
swifter than the sun. Swelling seas,
and the lap of the earth, the green fields,
are within my clasp. I cover the depths,
and plunge beneath hell; I ascend above heaven,
highland of glory; I stretch across
the region of angels; I fill the earth
with myself – this whole middle-earth
and the ocean streams. Say what my name is.

69

On the way a miracle: water become bone.

This creature is odd, its habits unaccountable.
It sings through its sides. Its neck is curved,
skilfully carved, and above its back
it has pointed shoulders. It plays its fated part
as, gracefully, it stands by the roadside,
high and handsome, useful to men.

72

[*lines* 1–5*a defective*]

    . . . often I pulled at four
sweet brothers; each plied me
with drink day by day, it poured
through separate holes. I drank, happy,
until I was older and yielded it all
to the dark herdsman; I left home,
trudged over the Marches, crossed the moors,
yoked under a beam with a ring around my neck –
every step was such drudgery,
a measure of hardship. Often the iron
gashed my sides grievously; I kept
quiet, never complained to any man
if the spear-stabs were painful.

74

I was once a young woman,
a glorious warrior, a grey-haired queen.
I soared with birds, stepped on the earth,
swam in the sea – dived under waves,
languid amongst fishes. I had a living spirit.

76

I saw a woman, solitary, brooding.

77

Sea suckled me, waves sounded over me,
rollers covered me as I rested on my bed.
I have no feet and often open my mouth
to the flood. Now some man will
consume me, who cares nothing for my clothing.
With the point of his knife he will rip the skin
away from my side, and straight away eat me
uncooked as I am . . .

80

I'm loved by my lord, and his shoulder
companion, I'm the comrade of a warrior,
a friend of the King. The fair-haired
Queen, the daughter of an earl, sometimes lays
her hand on me, well-born though she is.
I carry within me what grew in the grove.
Sometimes I ride on a splendid steed
at the head of the host; harsh is my voice.
I often give the singer a reward
for his songs. I'm sallow to look at
and kind at heart. What am I called?

81

My breast is puffed up, my neck is swollen.
I've a fine head and a high waving tail,
ears and eyes also but only one foot;
a long neck, a strong beak, a back and
two sides, and a rod right through my middle.
My home is high above men. When he who stirs
the forest moves me, I suffer misery.
Scourged by the rainlash, I stand alone;
I am bruised by batteries of hail,
hoar-frost attacks and snow half-hides me.
I must endure all this, not pour out my misery.

83

My origin was age-old [I endured many winters];
I lived in towns after the keeper of fire
[unlocked the lives] of men encircled by flame,
purged by fire. Now the brother of earth,
my enemy, who from the first brought me
sorrow, imprisons me. I well remember
who drew me and my like from our first
abode; I can do him no evil
but at times I'm an instrument of bondage
the whole world over. I've many talents,
on middle-earth I've vast strength,
but I must conceal from all men
the secret source of my precious skill
and my extraction. Guess what I'm called.

84

On earth there's a creature wondrously conceived:
she's wild and unruly, unbridled her momentum;
she roars fiercely as she rolls across the earth.
She has mothered many splendid creatures.
This fair traveller is always eager,
headstrong and inescapable. No one can find
the fitting words to describe to others
her splendid appearance, her innumerable kin,
her ancient origin; the Father saw it all,
the beginning and end, and so did the Son,
sublime child of the Creator . . .
[*lines 11b–20 defective or missing*]
This mother is endowed with massive strength;
wondrously sustained, teeming with food
and treasure-adorned, she's dear to men.
Her force increases, her might is revealed,
her grace enhanced by the great good she offers –
a gift refreshing for proud people,
she's pure and bountiful, boundless her excellence.
She's precious to the rich, useful to the poor,
priceless and freeborn; of all things created
under the sky, on which the sons of men
have set eyes, she's the strongest,
the most strenuous as she covers the ground,
the most grasping and most greedy (so lives
this glorious creature, kinswoman of mortals),
although keen in mind . . .
a more discerning man, a host of marvels.
She's harder than earth, older than heroes,

more generous than gold-givers, dearer than gems;
she beautifies the world, gives birth
to plants, washes away suffering.
From outside, she casts a veil –
a marvellous making – over countless people,
and on earth everywhere men gaze in wonder . . .
[*lines* 43–56 *defective*]

85

My home's not silent, but I am not
loud-mouthed. The Lord shaped
our course together: I'm swifter than he,
sometimes stronger; he's more strenuous.
At times I rest; he must run onward.
But I live in him all the days of my life;
if we're divided I'm certain to die.

86

A creature came where there sat
many wise men in the meeting-place.
He had two ears and one eye,
two feet and twelve hundred heads,
a back and a belly, a pair of hands,
two shoulders and arms, a neck,
and two sides. Now tell me his name.

91

My head was hammered into shape, scarred
by sharp chisels, scoured by a file.
I often gape at what faces me
when wearing rings, I thrust firmly
against a hard object; hollowed out
from behind, I strain at what stands between
my lord and his heart's desire at midnight.
Sometimes I pull back my nose,
guardian of gold, when my murderous lord
plans to steal treasures from those whom he
has had disposed of, just as he pleases.

93

[*lines 1–8 defective*]

At times he would spring up the steep slopes
in his own fells, at times plunge
into deep dales, with great leaps,
in search of food; he kicked up frozen
scree, sometimes he shook the frost
from his ashen hair.

              With the eager ones I rode
until my younger brother usurped my position
(happy it was) and drove me from my home.
After that an iron weapon, gleaming,
gashed my stomach; although the sharp-edged steel
bit into me savagely, no blood, no gore,
issued from me. I did not mourn that hour
nor weep at my wound, nor was I able
to avenge my misery with a warrior's life;
rather, I suffer pain from all those
that have bitten the shield. Now I swallow black –
wood and water – and in my womb encircle
something dark that (as I stand here)
falls on me from above; I have one foot.
Now the preying foe, who once carried
the wolf's companion far and wide,
pilfers my treasure; it often sallies
out of my stomach, the stout table . . .

[*lines 32–35 defective*]

95

I am noble and known to warriors,
and often rest; renowned amongst men
(high and humble), I range far and wide,
and plunderers' pickings are mine if I,
once estranged from friends, can but win
success and shining reward in halls.
Now clever men greatly welcome
my presence; I'll reveal wisdom
to many people; no one on earth
speaks a word. Although sons of men,
livers on land, now eagerly watch
for some sign of me, I sometimes
hide my tracks from all humankind.

NOTES

Riddle 1

The *Exeter Book* riddles begin with a dramatic description of
a storm. There has been much discussion as to whether lines
1–74 constitute one, two or three riddles; but the scribe has
divided his material into three parts, and I have elected to
follow him. The invitation in the closing lines of Riddles 1
and 2 follows a convention often used to round off the riddles,
and strongly suggests that we are dealing with three separate
entities, but on the other hand the last paragraph of Riddle 3
appears to be a recapitulation of all that has gone before. The
solution to this first riddle is generally taken to be *storm on
land*, but this and the following two riddles are not really
enigmatic; they are fine descriptive poems. Lines 12–14 refer
to the Old Testament Flood.

Riddle 2

Commentators have accepted that the answer to this riddle
(or part of a riddle) is *submarine earthquake*. It could, however,
be *storm at sea*.

Riddle 3

These forceful lines describe an earthquake, a storm at sea,
and a thunderstorm back on land. The most sensible blanket
designation is *storm*. The word 'shrithing' in line 50 derives
from the Old English *scriþan*, meaning a sinewy and sinister
gliding movement; it is also used by the *Beowulf*-poet in

describing both the monster Grendel and the dragon. The Anglo-Saxons' love and fear of the sea is conveyed as well in these lines as anywhere in Old English literature. The 'flint-grey rollers', the 'spines of breakers' and the 'yells of sailors' are the phrases of a man who has really visualized these things.

Riddle 4

Millstone, *flail* and *lock* have their advocates, but *bell* is the most favoured solution to this riddle. Cathedrals and leading churches in Anglo-Saxon England may not have boasted teams of campanologists but some were certainly equipped with a bell or bells: a page from the tenth-century *Benedictional of St Æthelwold* shows the Saint blessing a congregation from the door of the new cathedral at Winchester which he had rebuilt in 980, and the cathedral is furbished with a splendid bell-tower with three bells; it is also crowned with a weathercock (see Riddle 81).

Riddle 5

Shield. The rune for S, which can represent either *scyld* or *scutum* (shield) is written beneath this riddle, the first of several in the *Exeter Book* concerned with weaponry. The circular or kite-shaped curved shield of wood, covered with hide with an iron boss, was the most common weapon of defence. Nothing portrays as vividly as the Bayeux Tapestry the way in which the shield stood – or failed to stand – between man and sword, man and axe, and, as the *Beowulf*-poet says, man and 'the iron-tipped arrow-shower'.

Riddle 6

Sun. As a kind of extra clue, the same rune that closes Riddle 5 closes this riddle too; in this instance it is thought to represent either *sigel* or *sol* (sun). No matter what the riddler says, Anglo-Saxon summers were not tropical, but much of a muchness with those experienced in Britain today.

Riddle 7

Swan. This riddle touches on the classical tradition that the swan has musical plumage, in that harmony and sweetness are produced by the breath of the West wind against its wings. And most musically it begins:

> Hraegl min swigeð,   þonne ic hrusan trede,
> oþþe þa wic buge,   oþþe wado drefe.

These and the following lines (the first that I translated from Old English, having just been attacked by a swan) foreshadow that great poem by W. B. Yeats, 'The Wild Swans at Coole':

> But now they drift on the still water,
> Mysterious, beautiful;
> Among what rushes will they build,
> By what lake's edge or pool
> Delight man's eyes when I awake some day
> To find they have flown away?

Riddle 8

Commentators dispute the answer to this riddle with the voices of Babel: *nightingale, wood-pigeon, chough, jackdaw, bell* (most unconvincingly) have been suggested, but *jay*, first proposed by Frederick Tupper, seems the most likely solution. This riddle and Riddle 24 (which contains its own answer, *bigora* – jay or magpie) have much in common. I find the picture of men at the day's end who 'sit, bowed down, quiet in their houses' moving in its contrast to the songbird's unabashed vigour.

Riddle 9

Cuckoo. Here is the familiar, cruel story of the fledgling cuckoo, told in a charming way. Several references to the bird in Old English literature capitalize on the paradox that its two-toned song is the melancholy announcement of something gay.

> And the cuckoo, harbinger of summer, sings
> a mournful song, boding bitter sorrow
> to the heart . . .
>
> ('The Seafarer')

Riddle 10

Speculation that the answer to this riddle might be *ocean-furrow* or *bubble* or *anchor* or *water-lily* have given way to a consensus that the right solution is *barnacle goose*, first proposed by Stopford Brooke in his *History of Early English Literature*. The barnacle goose (*Anas leucopsis*), a species of wild goose that breeds in the Arctic and visits Britain in winter, was once thought to be produced out of a barnacle shell, while another school of thought held that barnacle geese grew on trees, to which they were attached by their bills. In the twelfth century Giraldus Cambrensis noted:

Bernacae are like marsh-geese, but somewhat smaller. They are produced from fir-timber tossed along the sea, and are at first like gum. Afterwards they hang down by their beaks, as if from a seaweed attached to the timber, surrounded by shells in order to grow more freely. Having thus in process of time been clothed with a strong coat of feathers, they either fall into the water or fly freely away into the air.

Riddle 11

Four solutions, *wine*, *beaker of wine*, *night* and *gold*, have been proposed. The internal evidence of the poem (especially lines 5b–8) and the similarities to Riddle 27 (*mead*) make *wine* the most likely. The crucial penultimate line appears to have been wrongly copied by the *Exeter Book* scribe and has provoked much argument: a small emendation enables one to translate it as I have done, in which case the 'dearest of hoards' may refer to the soul; a larger emendation allows the literal translation, 'when the dearest of hoards (the sun) hastens on high', leading to the solution *night*.

The Anglo-Saxons drank mead and ale day-in, day-out, and there are many references to both drinks in their literature. Wine was a rarer commodity, and a pupil in Ælfric's *Colloquy*, a dialogue used in monastery schools to teach Latin, comments, 'I'm not rich enough to buy myself wine; and wine isn't a drink for children or the foolish, but for the old and wise.' There were some vineyards in the South of England and much wine was imported from France and Germany in large *amphorae* and in wooden barrels like those depicted in the Bayeux Tapestry. When the merchant in the same *Colloquy* is asked what he brings to England, he replies: 'Purple garments and silks; precious gems and gold, strange raiment and spice; wine and oil; ivory and brass; copper and tin; sulphur and glass, and many such things . . .'

Riddle 12

Leather, depicted first on the living ox, then made into thongs, into a gourd, and into shoes. There are analogues in the four Latin riddle collections with which the *Exeter Book* riddler was familiar. In particular, the last two lines are very close to the end of Eusebius' Riddle 37 (*calf*): 'And if I live, I begin to

plough up hills; or if I die, I bind up many who are alive.'
The Old English word *wealh* (lines 3 and 7) means 'Welshman',
'Cornishman', 'slave' and 'shameless one' – a reflection of the
old bitter conflict between Celt and Saxon in the fifth and
sixth centuries, when many Britons were taken into slavery.
Consider the wars of the Middle Ages, the long tormented
history of Ireland, the present nationalist parties and policies;
in many ways, the struggle still continues. In the words of
R. S. Thomas:

> We are not English . . . *Ni bydd diwedd*
> *Byth ar sŵn y delyn aur.*
> Though the strings are broken, and time sets
> The barbed wire in their place,
> The tune endures; on the cracked screen
> Of life our shadows are large still
> In history's fierce afterglow.
>
> ('Border Blues')

(The Welsh words mean 'There will never be an end to the
sound of the golden harp.')

Riddle 13

The solution *ten chickens* is widely but not universally accepted.
Mrs von Erhardt-Siebold explains the six brothers and their
sisters by pointing out that in Old English ten chickens, *ten
ciccenu*, has six consonants and four vowels. When it is hatched,
a chick leaves its membrane clinging to the inside of the shell.

Riddle 14

Horn. This is the more elaborate and perhaps less poetically
satisfying of the two 'horn' riddles (the other is Riddle 80) in
the *Exeter Book*. The horn lived first on the head of the

auroch or wild ox. Great herds once roamed through the forests of north-west Europe but the animal became extinct five or six hundred years ago. Then the horn was decorated and used to hold wine (on average, it held three or four pints), or to summon men to battle.

Riddle 15

Badger is the most widely accepted solution, although a case has also been made out for *porcupine* (known to Anglo-Saxons as *se mara igil*, 'the larger hedgehog'), *fox* and *hedgehog*. There are many textual difficulties and, consequently, opportunities for different interpretation. Stopford Brooke observed: 'It is in these short poems – in this sympathetic treatment of the beasts of the wood, as afterwards of the birds; in this transference to them of human passions and of the interest awakened by their suffering and pleasure – that the English poetry of animals begins'.

Riddle 16

Anchor. This riddle is an elaboration of Symphosius' Riddle 61 (*anchor*): 'My twin points are joined by a single bar of iron. I struggle with the wind; I fight with the deep sea. I probe into the middle of the waters; I also bite the earth itself.'

Riddle 17

Ballista, *fortress* and *oven* have been advocated as solutions; the similarities between this riddle and Riddle 23, which declares itself to be a bow, make *ballista* the most likely solution. Used by Greeks, Romans and many other early cultures, the *ballista* is 'an ancient military engine, resembling a bow stretched with cord and thongs, used to hurl stones, etc.'.

Riddle 18

I'm a strange creature; I can't speak a word,
amuse men with talk, although I've a mouth,
a massive paunch . . .

*

I was on a ship with my family

These three and a half lines are all that survive of what must have been a longer riddle, although no loss is indicated in the manuscript. The last line appears to belong to some other riddle. One commentator, Dietrich, has volunteered *leather bottle* as a solution; he may be right, but it is worth noting the object in question has the same 'massive paunch' ascribed to *bellows* in Riddles 37 and 87.

Riddle 19

On my way I saw S R O
H so spirited, with gleaming mane,
galloping hard across the green plain.
On its back it bore battle-might;
N O M without a weapon rode
A G E W. Ranging far, fleet of foot
on its journey, it carried a keen C O
F O A H. The way, the track of these travellers
was the more noble. Guess my name.

This riddle is dominated by four runic groups which read SROH, NOM, AGEW (probably) and COFOAH. Read backwards, we have the Old English words *hors*, *mon*, *wega* and *haofoc* – 'horse', 'man', 'ways', and 'hawk'. It is impossible to say more than that this riddle, and its companion Riddle 64, revolve around these four constituents; there does not appear to be an answer as such. Since the riddle seems too generalized to refer to some specific story, it may just have been a poet's test as to whether his audience were good *rynemenn*, 'runemen'.

Riddle 20

Sword is accepted by all commentators save one who takes the solution to be *hawk* or *falcon*. The riddle is incomplete, and Krapp and Dobbie, editors of *The Anglo-Saxon Poetic Records*, comment that 'the evidence of the gatherings reinforces the evidence of the text that a folio has been lost at this point, containing the remainder of Riddle 20 and probably some other riddles as well.' The conflict between the beautiful, chaste sword and the scold, resentful at her husband's lack of attention, is vivid and amusing, and it is a pity that only part of it survives.

To own a sword implied standing and wealth; maybe it was the mark of a thane. The most renowned of swords were important bequeathals (King Alfred mentions one in his will) and had lineages of famous owners; they also had names, such as 'Nægling', Beowulf's sword, which snapped in his fight against the dragon. The blades, almost a metre long, were sometimes engraved with ornamental patterning or with runes, like the sword found a Lincoln bearing the mysterious music ANTANANANTANANTAN, but the finest decoration (as this riddle indicates) was usually reserved for the hilt.

Riddle 21

Plough. The 'grey foe of the forest' could be either iron (which, as an axe, felled a tree) or, possibly the ploughman. The two sharp weapons are the share and coulter. The passage about the lot of the ploughman in Ælfric's *Colloquy* is charming and moving:

PLOUGHMAN: O Master, I work very hard; I go out at dawn, drive the oxen to the field, and yoke them to the plough. There is no storm so severe that I dare to hide at home, for fear of my lord, but when the oxen are yoked, and the share and coulter have been fastened to the plough, I must plough a whole acre or more every day.

TEACHER: Have you any companion?

PLOUGHMAN: I have a boy to urge on the oxen with a goad; he is now hoarse on account of the cold and his shouting.

TEACHER: What else do you do during the day?

PLOUGHMAN: I do a great deal more. I must fill the bins of the oxen with the hay, water them, and carry off their dung.

TEACHER: Oh! Oh! The labour must be great.

PLOUGHMAN: It is indeed great drudgery, because I am not free.

Riddle 22

Although some commentators believe that the answer to this riddle is *the circling stars* (or the Great Bear or Charles's Wain), and cite Aldhelm's riddle 'Arcturus' as a remote analogue, the evidence in favour of the solution, *the month of December*, seems to me to be conclusive. The 'sixty men' are the sixty half-days, or days and nights, of the month – there are many examples of the Anglo-Saxons' habit of counting in halves. The eleven men mounted on 'horses of peace' are the month's four Sundays and seven feast days (Conception of the Virgin, St Nicholas, St Thomas, Christmas, St Stephen, St John Evangelist, Holy Innocents). The water divides one year from the next and the 'opposite side' is therefore January. These ramifications are rather elaborate, but see the Introduction (p. x) for a discussion of the Time-Riddle.

Riddle 23

Bow. The first word of the riddle is *agof* which, read backwards, gives *foga* which is an earlier form of *boga*, bow. The archer was by no means a commonplace of Anglo-Saxon warfare. Indeed it was essentially the massed archers and cavalry who enabled the Normans to scrape home at Hastings.

Riddle 24

Jay, magpie. The runes in this riddle read G, Æ, R, O, H and I. This is an anagram of *higoræ* (= *higore*), which is the feminine form of *higora*, jay or magpie. These lines abound with ono-matopoeia: the dog *beorce*, barks; the goat *blaete*, bleats; the goose *graede*, honks; and the hawk *gielle* (pronounced 'yella'), shrieks.

Riddle 25

This is the first of seven 'obscene' riddles in the *Exeter Book*. The answer is *onion* (other suggestions have been *leek*, *hip* – fruit of the wild rose – *hemp* and *mustard*) and the innuendo-answer is *penis*. Apart from its success as *double entendre*, this and the other 'obscene' riddles show the Anglo-Saxon sense of humour to have been not only ironic (as many Old English poems demonstrate) but, as one might expect, earthy. It is worth reiterating that the *Exeter Book* was compiled for a bishop to donate to his cathedral library. Pious and ascetic the Anglo-Saxon monks were but, unlike some contemporary critics, they were not prim.

Riddle 26

Book, clearly religious, maybe a copy of the Gospels. The *Exeter Book* riddler was plainly aware of, but did not imitate,

Aldhelm's Riddles 32 and 59 (*writing-tablets* and *quill*) and Eusebius' Riddles 32 and 33 (*parchment* and *quill*).

The production of a book before the revolutionary invention of the printing press – surely the most significant invention of all time – was a lengthy business. Each monastery had its own scriptorium and, especially during the seventh and eighth centuries, Anglo-Saxon monasteries produced a steady stream of books – copies of the scriptures, biblical exegeses, treatises on grammar, natural science, chronology, lives of the saints, and so forth – for use at home and abroad. A touching letter from Abbot Cuthbert of Wearmouth in 773 to a continental bishop who had asked for copies of Bede's works has something to say about the scribe's working conditions: 'And if I could have done more I would gladly have done so. For the conditions of the past winter oppressed the island of our race very horribly with cold and ice and long and widespread storms of wind and rain, so that the hand of the scribe was hindered from producing a great number of books.'

The Roman Catholic church has always maintained that no expense or effort should be spared over objects made to the greater glory of God, and there are few greater glories than the best Anglo-Saxon illuminated manuscripts, such as the *Lindisfarne Gospels*. Far from simply acting as copyists, the ascetic monks decorated their functional manuscripts inside and out with a grand, controlled passion: the vellum pages, glowing with solid mineral colours, red lead, bluish green (extracted from malachite), bright yellow (extracted from arsenic salts), and pink, blue, purple, brown and gold, are works of art of the very highest order.

This riddle occupies an extraordinary place in our literature. It was composed to be recited, and yet it celebrates something that is read. It stands at the crossroads of the oral and written traditions.

Riddle 27

Mead. A thane's wife was responsible for the brewing of ale and the making of mead, which consists of water and fermented honey and was stored in urns. It is extremely strong but rather sickly, and was doubtless diluted. Honey was the only form of sweetening known to the Anglo-Saxons and consequently bees and the art of bee-keeping were highly prized. A charm survives, words once spoken to restrain bees:

> *When they swarm, scatter earth over them and say:*
> 'Alight, victorious women, alight on the earth!
> Never turn wild and fly to the woods!
> Be just as mindful of my benefit
> As is every man of his food and fatherland.'

Riddle 28

Although some commentators have proposed *wine-cask* and *harp*, the evidence is overwhelmingly in favour of *John Barleycorn* or *ale*. In making my translation I have leant heavily on John Seymour's admirable description of the process of harvesting and malting barley and making ale (fermented malt) in *The Complete Book of Self-Sufficiency* (Faber, 1976). My version of lines 4–6 to some extent simplifies the original – but then a word like 'sparging' is not common coin in the way its equivalent was to the Anglo-Saxons. There is unfortunately no way in which a translator can echo the remarkable music (achieved by adding rhyming pairs to the usual alliteration and four-stress lines) of this same passage:

> corfen, sworfen,   cyrred, þyrred,
> bunden, wunden,   blaeced, waeced,
> fraetwed, geatwed,   feorran laeded
> to durum dryhta.

Riddle 29

Moon and sun is widely accepted, although a case has also been made out for *swallow and sparrow*, *bird and wind* and *cloud and wind*. The concept that the moon has horns and plunders the sun's light has the quality and weight of myth; this seems to me a most successful riddle and an appropriately mysterious and haunting poem.

Riddle 30a

For some reason there are two widely separated, virtually identical texts of Riddle 30 in the *Exeter Book*. I have followed the example of Krapp and Dobbie in *The Anglo-Saxon Poetic Records* in designating them Riddles 30a and 30b. (Riddle 30b follows Riddle 59). There has been much discussion as to the composite parts of the solution, but it is agreed that the riddle is a pun on the Old English word *beam*, which carried a number of meanings. The meaning 'tree' suits lines 1b–2 and 3b–4a; the meaning 'ship' fits line 3a, 'log' lines 1a and 4b, and 'cup' lines 5–6. In the last three lines Christ's Cross (*beam* also means wood) speaks in the first person, as it does in the finest of the Old English religious poems, 'The Dream of the Rood'.

Riddle 31

Bagpipe is almost universally accepted. In this charming and effective portrayal of the instrument as a rather helpless, dumb bird who 'makes sense only with her dangling foot', the beak is the chanter and the brothers are the drones. Paradoxically, the hoard in line 21 consists of nothing but air, with which the bag is inflated. Writing in the sixth century, Procopius refers to the bagpipe as the war instrument of Roman

infantry. Horn and harp often appear in manuscript illumi-
nation and poem, and remains of them have been unearthed in
archaeological discoveries – perhaps there were as few Anglo-
Saxons unable to play a stringed instrument and recite a
poem as there are people in Britain and America today unable
to read – but references to other musical instruments are
infrequent.

Riddle 32

Probably *ship*. *Wheel*, *millstone* and *wagon* have also been sug-
gested. Krapp and Dobbie comment that 'the vessel described
in the riddle is one of the decked merchant ships of the late
Anglo-Saxon period, the *muð*, line 9, being the hatchway.'

Riddle 33

Iceberg. The riddler was probably working on hearsay, for
icebergs were seen no further south than they are today. In
The Art of Poesie (1589), Puttenham wrote:

We dissemble again under covert and dark speeches, when we speak
by way of riddle (*Enigma*) of which the sense can hardly be picked
out, but by the parties owne assoile, as he that said:
> 'It is my mother well I wot
> And yet the daughter that I begot!'.
Meaning by it the ise which is made of frozen water, the same, being
molten by the sunne or fire, makes water again.

Riddle 34

Rake. The object described is mundane but the treatment is
sensitive and the atmospheric ending unforced.

Riddle 35

Coat of mail. This is quite a close translation of Aldhelm's
Riddle 33; and at the end of a collection of Aldhelm's riddles
in Leiden University Library there is another version of this
riddle, written in Northumbrian dialect. The device of sol-
ution by elimination makes for a most effective riddle.

Riddle 36

> I saw a creature riding over the rollers,
> it was adorned with curious ornaments.
> It had four feet beneath its stomach
> and eight –
> man . hwm . woman . mxlkfwf . horse . qxxs .
>   – on its back;
> it had two wings, twelve eyes,
> and six heads. Say what it was.
> It surged over the swell; and it was not
> a bird alone, for it bore the likeness
> of a horse, a man and a hound, also
> the shape of a woman. You who are able
> to ascertain the answer can spell out
> this creature's name, and explain its nature.

'This is one of the riddles', wrote A. J. Wyatt, 'one
wishes at the bottom of the Bay of Portugal: there is no
poetry in it, and the ingenuity is misplaced.' *Ship* is com-
monly accepted as the solution, but this should really be
extended to *a ship with three passengers* or some such if lines
7–12 are taken into account. Interpretations of these lines
differ: perhaps Frederick Tupper's argument is the most con-
vincing – namely, that the four feet are oars and the eight
'on its back' are the feet of the man, woman and horse on
deck. He continues, 'The horse, man, dog, bird, and
woman, of which it bears the likeness (i.e. which it carries),

supply, if we add the ship's figurehead, the two wings, twelve eyes, and six heads.'

It is thought that line 5 was a marginal note and not originally part of the riddle; it is not as complicated as it looks, but is simply written in a code in which each vowel is represented by the consonant in the alphabet that follows it. The scribe, however, has slipped up and both miscopied and misplaced the cryptic lettering, which, decoded, should actually read, *bomo*, *mulier* and *equus*, each repeating the Old English word that precedes it.

Riddle 37

This is one of two riddles (the other is Riddle 87) to which the answer is *bellows*, and with a certain amount of *double entendre* it wittily develops Symphosius' Riddle 73, which reads: 'I do not die immediately when the breath leaves, for it returns continually; although it often departs again too. At one time my soul's power is considerable; at another, it is nothing.' The last line means that the bellows gives birth to air (as it pumps it out), yet also gives itself air and life (as it draws air in).

Riddle 38

Young bull. The bullock drinks at its mother's four teats. Alive, it breaks ground with the plough; dead, its hide forms thongs. Traditionally, it was with a thong that Hengest (a Saxon mercenary) first established himself in England after Vortigern had asked for his assistance. In the words of that unreliable twelfth-century historian Geoffrey of Monmouth, Hengest says: 'Grant me, then, as much land as can be encircled by a thong.' Vortigern agrees and Hengest 'then took the hide of a bull and cut it into a single leather thong. With this thong he marked out a certain precipitous site, which he had chosen with the greatest possible cunning. Inside the space which he had measured he began to build a fortress.'

Riddle 39

Time, *day* and *moon* have been proposed, but line 20, 'It has never thrust to heaven', appears to rule out *moon*. In line 14, I have taken the emendation *earuwost*, 'most swift', which makes better sense than *earmost*, 'most wretched'.

Riddle 40

Creation. This is much the longest riddle in the collection and, even so, it is incomplete because a leaf is missing between folios 111 and 112 of the *Exeter Book*. It is a translation of Aldhelm's Riddle 100, *De Creatura*. Paull F. Baum notes that the Anglo-Saxon poet generally needed two lines for each hexameter and adds: 'This use of two lines for one is responsible for the thinness of the style.' It is true that there are some limp lines, some *longueurs* and some difficulties with the Latin (though few translators will think it wise to rail at another's howler!), notably the invention of the 'pernex' in line 64, where the poet misunderstood *plus pernex aquilis* ('swifter than the eagle') and took the adjective to be the name of a bird; but this riddle is also packed out with memorable images and vivid contrasts, and at times achieves a degree of real authority.

Riddle 41

Only the last eight and a half lines of the riddle survive; it began on the missing folio (see note to Riddle 40). No translation is offered because these lines provide no basis for a solution and are of little poetic consequence. They refer to an object which is the mother of many children, who are the 'best' and 'darkest' and 'dearest' owned by men, and say that we must 'enjoy what the children of men do' if we are to live on earth at all. *Wisdom* and three of the elements – *earth*, *fire* and *water* – have been tentatively advanced as answers.

Riddle 42

Cock and hen. Rearranged, the runes read *hana*, 'cock', and *hæn*, 'hen'. Lines 10b to 14a are rather involved; the poet was perhaps straining too hard after effects.

Riddle 43

Soul and body. The 'noble guest' is the soul; its servant and brother is the body. The earth is mother and sister to them both – mother because man's body is made of dust, and sister because she was made by the same father, God. The nature and relationship of the soul and body is also the subject of several longer Anglo-Saxon texts.

Riddle 44

Most leading commentators accept the answer *key*, but the innuendo-answer is obviously *penis*. The first lines are promisingly suggestive, but overall this riddle is not sufficiently ambiguous to avoid crudity.

Riddle 45

Dough, leavened with an ounce or two of *double entendre*.

Riddle 46

Lot with his two daughters and their sons. *Genesis* 19:30–38 tells how Lot feared to live in Zoar and went to live with his profligate daughters in a mountain cave; there they twice made him drunk and each seduced him. 'Thus were both the daughters of Lot with child by their father.' One bore Moab, and the other Ben-ammi. The first use of this incestuous story for the purpose of a riddle is attributed to the Queen of Sheba; she tried it on Solomon.

Riddle 47

Bookmoth. The source for these charming lines is Symphosius' Riddle 16, 'Tinea', wittily translated by Richard Wilbur:

> Illiterate, on letters have I dined;
> I've lived in books but not improved my mind;
> Devoured the Muses, and still am unrefined.

Riddle 48

The answer to this riddle is some kind of church plate: either *chrismal*, *paten* or *chalice*. It has similarities to Riddle 59. The Romans mined gold, famous for its red lustre, at Dolaucothi in Carmarthenshire. It sounds as if this object was fashioned from ore from the same source. Many Anglo-Saxon gold objects were made from melted and re-cycled Roman coins.

Riddle 49

Book-case is held to be the most likely solution, but *falcon-cage* and *oven* have also been suggested; Aldhelm's Riddle 89 has been cited as an analogue. Very few individuals would have possessed books of their own, let alone the 'twenty book, clad in blak or reed' later preferred by Chaucer's Clerk of Oxenford; most manuscripts belonged to the monasteries where they were written, illuminated and bound (see note to Riddle 26), or else to cathedral libraries.

Riddle 50

Most critics accept the solution *fire*. The 'two dumb creatures' must be flints, or pieces of steel, or possibly even pieces of wood.

Riddle 51

Pen and three fingers is widely accepted, in which case the 'four curious creatures' can be explained as the thumb, two fingers and pen, a quill which as a feather had once supported the swift bird; the 'toiling warrior' would be either the mind or the arm of the scribe; and the 'gold' may refer to manuscript illumination or possibly to inlay on the ink-horn (subject of Riddles 88 and 93). Less convincing cases have also been made out for the solutions *dragon* and *horse and waggon*.

The *Exeter Book* itself is written in a generous, attractive hand and is generally supposed to be the work of one scribe. Krapp and Dobbie note: 'The variations which we find in the writing of the *Exeter Book* are by no means too great to be explained as a result of variations in the quality of the parchment and the use of different pens.'

Riddle 52

The commonly accepted solution is *flail*, although *well-buckets* and *a yoke of oxen led into a barn by a female slave* and *broom* have had their advocates. The two 'violent captives' can be interpreted as the flail's handle and swingle.

Riddle 53

Battering-ram. The Anglo-Saxons were very conscious of the power and beauty of trees, and of their use and abuse by men. The *lance* (Riddle 73) alludes to fierce foes that first cut it down when it was a tree; the *bow* (Riddle 23) refers to its torment; and the *plough* (Riddle 21) speaks of its many scars. And, in 'The Dream of the Rood', the tree hewn into the Cross says:

> 'I remember the morning a long time ago
> that I was felled at the edge of the forest
> and severed from my roots. Strong enemies
> seized me and fashioned me for their sport,
> bade me hold up their felons on high.'

Riddle 54

This is one of the more witty and successful of the *double entendre* riddles. A nice balance is struck between the proper answer, *churn*, and the innuendo-answer which could perhaps be designated *coition*.

Riddle 55

The editors of *The Anglo-Saxon Poetic Records* put paid to *shield*, *scabbard*, *gallows*, *cross* and *harp*, and demonstrate that *sword-rack* must be the solution. The object is portrayed in the shape of both cross and gallows, and is made of four kinds of timber as the Cross was often said to have been. The paradox of the tree that is decorated with gold, silver and jewels and yet causes suffering and death is developed more fully in 'The Dream of the Rood' (see notes to Riddles 30a and 53).

Riddle 56

Probably *loom*. The 'struggling creature' is the web and the 'spears' have been explained by Mrs von Erhardt-Siebold as 'the teeth of a batten penetrating through the warp'. The 'bright leaves' probably refer to flax on a distaff.

Riddle 57

There is now general agreement that the solution is likely to be some species of bird (thereby disposing of the earlier proposals, *hail-stones*, *rain-drops* and *gnats*), but it is impossible to say which. *Swallows*, *starlings*, *jackdaws* and *crows* have been advocated, and it seems to me that the internal evidence of the poem also makes *house-martins* a possibility. There is a charming springy lift to the original, which begins:

> þeos lyft byreð   lytle wihte
> ofer beorghleoþa.   þa sind blace swiþe,
> swearte salopade.

Riddle 58

Draw-well is the commonly accepted answer to this riddle, but these lines in fact describe only the *well-sweep* – the long pole attached to an upright, with a bucket hanging on its end. In the last line, the relation of *Rad* to the solution has caused problems; some critics think that the scribe made an error and that the word should read *Rod*, an upright pole, but *Rad* (riding, journey) is quite appropriate. The identity of the other two 'fitting runes' can only be guessed at – a game for academics.

Riddle 59

This is the second and more long-winded of the two riddles concerning church plate (the other is Riddle 48) and most critics accept the solution *chalice*. The turning of the ring (line 5) has not been explained satisfactorily; it probably refers to the holding of the chalice (and by inference the drinking of Christ's blood) and perhaps to the act of passing it to the next communicant.

Riddle 30b

See note to Riddle 30a. The textual differences between the two riddles are very small; the translation is identical.

Riddle 60

These lines precede the text of 'The Husband's Message', a poem in which a rune-stave speaks, asking a woman to sail south and join her exiled husband; some critics believe that they in fact constitute the first part of that poem, but I have followed the editors of *The Anglo-Saxon Poetic Records* in taking them to be a separate riddle. *Reed* seems the obvious answer – growing on a lonely shore, cut into a flute, and used as a pen. The riddle has similarities to Symphosius' Riddle 2: 'I am the riverbank's sweet mistress and the deep water's neighbour; I sing softly to the Muses. When I am bathed in black and grasped by a scholar's fingers, I am the tongue's messenger.'

Riddle 61

Helmet, or maybe *kirtle*, is the proper answer and *vagina* is the innuendo-answer.

Riddle 62

This riddle has made some commentators squirm. *Gimlet*, *burning arrow*, *poker* and *brand* have been suggested; but although this kind of sidetrack is clearly intended, the answer *penis* is unambiguous. Line 5–6a refer to masturbation rather than an oiled tow wrapped round an arrow or a piece of cloth round a burning poker. The implication of 'southerner' in line 6 has not been established; some critics think the word *superne* means simply a foreign man, or a servant; someone, anyhow, whose behaviour is un-English!

Riddle 63

The text of the second half of this riddle is too defective to translate. The first half is intact and reads:

> I must often (and gracefully) gratify
> retainers in the hall when I'm taken round,
> gleaming with gold, where warriors carouse.
> Sometimes in the closet, when we're on our own,
> a loyal servant kisses my mouth;
> with his fingers he presses, embraces me,
> he works his will . . .

A *drinking-vessel* of some sort is clearly intended, and the riddle also contains sexual innuendo. Aldhelm's Riddle 80, *glass wine-cup*, has been cited as an analogue. Part of it reads: 'Many men want to clasp my neck with their right hands and to hold my slippery body in their fingers. But when I bring sweet kisses to their lips, laying them on the mouths which press close to me, I upset their minds and bring their staggering footsteps to a fall.'

Riddle 64

This riddle is six lines long and contains fifteen runes. It is clearly a companion to Riddle 19 in as much as the basic constituents are a man and his hawk. No translation is offered, for the meaning of some of the runes and the solution to the riddle are enigmatic in the extreme, and the riddle is also unsatisfying as a poem.

Riddle 65

Onion. This short riddle is as successful in its own way as its 'pair', Riddle 25. The original is attractively staccato:

Cwico waes ic, ne cwaeð ic wiht   cwele ic efne seþeah.
Ær ic waes, eft ic cwom.   Æghwa mec reafað,
hafað mec on headre,   ond min heafod scireþ . . .

Symphosius' Riddle 40 is a probable source: 'I bite those who bite me; otherwise I don't bite anyone. But many people are prepared to bite me who bite them. No one is afraid of my bite, since I don't have any teeth.'

Riddle 66

Creation. These lines incorporate some of the ideas and images developed in Riddle 40.

Riddle 67

I've heard of something concerning God,
a marvellous creature, mysterious words . . .
[*lines* 3–8 *defective*]
         . . . I've become
a teacher of nations. For which reason now
. . . I may live life everlasting
in diverse places, for as long as men
roam about earth's quarters. I've seen it
often, adorned with gold, treasure, silver,
where men sat drinking. Let him who can –
the most discerning – say what this object is.

The middle part of the riddle is too defective to be translated. The surviving lines suggest the solution *Bible*.

Riddle 68

All but two critics take Riddles 68 and 69 to be one riddle, with an answer involving the idea of running water becoming ice. But in *The Anglo-Saxon Poetic Records*, Krapp and Dobbie point out that 'they are written as separate riddles in the MS, and there is nothing in the texts of the two riddles which would justify us in associating them.' The two lines of this riddle are:

I watched a creature going on its way;
its clothes were as fine as they were curious.

They closely resemble the opening lines of Riddle 36 and are perhaps the start of a riddle the remainder of which was overlooked by the scribe, or already lost.

Riddle 69

Probably *ice*. See note to Riddle 68.

Riddle 70

Shepherd's pipe or *harp*. If line 2a refers to the holes for finger-
ing, the answer is likely to be a shepherd's pipe; but lines
2b–4a favour harp.

Riddle 71

> A rich man owns me, red gold clothes me.
> Once I was a tough, steep place, the station
> of shining flowers; now I'm the leavings
> of fire and file, firmly fastened,
> embellished with wire thread. He who thrusts
> against the gold will sometimes grieve
> at my onslaught when I, adorned with rings,
> smash [an heirloom] . . .

The text of the last two-and-a-half lines of this riddle is too
damaged to be translated. A. J. Wyatt's description of this
riddle as '*iron, first in the ore then made into a weapon*', is unlikely
to be bettered. There has been much inconclusive discussion
as to whether the 'tough steep place' in line 2 refers to the
blade itself or to the precipitous site from which the ore was
quarried.

Riddle 72

The text of lines 1–5a of this riddle is defective. *Ox* is widely
accepted as the solution, although an argument has been made
for *axle and wheels*.

Riddle 73

Lines 9–21 of this riddle are damaged and, although there is no break in the manuscript, the sense in line 24 suggests a word or two has been lost. The surviving lines read:

> I grew and lived in a field, where soil
> and the clouds of heaven fed me, until,
> when I was old, fierce enemies
> changed me from what I'd been, alive;
> they altered my estate, moved me from the earth
> and, against my nature, made me
> bow at times to the will of butchers.
> Now in my master's hands I'm busy . . .
> [*lines 9–21 defective*]
> cherishes me and in the skirmish fights
> with skilful control. Everyone knows
> that I'm one of the daring, and deft
> as a thief, under the brain-house [. . .]
> Sometimes, in full sight, I streak
> towards a stronghold that was peaceful before.
> Fleet of foot, the warrior turns
> and hurries from that place – he's aware
> of my ways. Say what my name is.

Lance is accepted by all commentators except Moritz Trautmann, who prefers *battering-ram*. It is true that there are some similarities between this riddle and Riddle 53.

Riddle 74

Commentators have argued for *cuttlefish*, *water*, *siren* and *swan*. There is no way of clinching the case one way or other, but Frederick Tupper has certainly advanced an interesting case for *siren*:

The Siren is both aged and young: centuries old and yet with the face of a girl. It is not only a woman but sometimes a man. At an early period of the Middle Ages the Teutonic conception of a fish-woman or mermaid met and mingled with the classical idea of a bird-maiden ... Every student of myths knows that when Ulysses or the Argonauts had passed in safety, the Sirens threw themselves into the sea, and were transformed into rocks.

Riddle 75

I saw a quick one coursing down a track
DNUH

Like Riddle 68, this may be the beginning of a longer riddle now lost; and like Riddle 19, the answer is achieved by reversing the order of the runes, which in the text read DNLH. Mackie would solve as HæLeND, 'Saviour'. Every other commentator emends the L to U and reads HUND, 'dog'.

Riddle 76

Although Tupper has argued that this one-liner is most likely to be the beginning of a longer riddle, it reads very satisfactorily as it stands, with *hen* as the solution.

Riddle 77

Oyster. The text of the last half-line is damaged. The loquacious 'Fisherman' in Ælfric's *Colloquy* talks of catching 'eels and pike, minnows and turbot, trout and lampreys ... herrings and salmon, porpoises and sturgeon, oysters and crabs, mussels, winkles, cockles, plaice and flounders and lobsters, and many similar things'.

Riddle 78

Only about twenty scattered words survive of this damaged eight-line riddle, and their translation serves no purpose. But parallels between Riddle 77 and what survives of this riddle suggest that the solution is *oyster*.

Riddle 79

This consists of one line:

> I'm a lord's possession and pleasure.

This is either a variation of the first line of Riddle 80 which begins with the same words (*Ic eom æpelinges*, 'I am of a lord') or another incomplete riddle.

Riddle 80

Horn is now widely agreed on, but *falcon*, *hawk*, *spear* and *sword* have also been suggested. See note to Riddle 14.

Riddle 81

Most commentators accept *weathercock*, which, with a bell (see note to Riddle 4) and a sundial, was one of the trappings of a well-equipped church. The stoic melancholy of this cameo is essentially Anglo-Saxon and echoes the tone of longer elegiac poems, such as 'The Wanderer':

> Time and again at the day's dawning
> I must mourn all my afflictions alone.
> There is no one still living to whom I dare open
> the doors of my heart. I have no doubt
> that it is a noble habit for a man

to bind fast all his heart's feelings with silence,
whatever his impulse, his inclinations.

Riddle 82

Of the original six lines, four fragments remain. They read:

A creature is . . .
. . . quick, devours a great deal,

*

. . . skin nor flesh, on its feet goes

*

the meals of each man it must . . .

Clearly, no solution is possible; there is not really sufficient evidence to support Holthausen's suggestion, *crab*.

Riddle 83

Ore is widely accepted as the answer to this rather obscure riddle. The text of the first eight lines has been the subject of many emendations, and any translation of them will contain some degree of speculation (the postulated restorations are printed in square brackets). The 'keeper of fire' in lines 2 and 4–5 has been taken by some commentators to be Tubal-cain (Genesis 4:22), but it could equally be a reference to Surt, who, in Norse mythology, ruled over Muspellheim (the world of fire). He already existed at the creation, when the worlds of fire and ice merged in the great chasm of Ginnungagap and life was first engendered.

Riddle 84

Water. Lines 11b–20 and 43–56 are badly damaged and cannot be translated; there is also a break in the sense in line 34, and a half-line is thought to be missing. The last surviving lines are fresh but overall the riddle is repetitive and rather wooden.

Riddle 85

Fish and river. Symphosius' Riddle 12, *Flumen et Piscis*, is the probable source of this riddle. It reads: 'On earth there is a home that echoes again and again with a clear sound. The home itself resounds, but the silent guest [*or* host] makes no noise. Yet the guest [*or* host] and the home both run on together.'

Riddle 86

Most critics accept *one-eyed seller of garlic*. The riddle makes me recall the occasional Breton onion-seller now seen no longer on London streets, precarious on his bicycle, draped in his wares. Symphosius' Riddle 95 is taken to be a source: 'Now you can see what you can hardly believe; he has one eye but many thousands of heads. He sells what he has; where will he buy what he doesn't have?'

Riddle 87

I saw a strange creature; it had a huge stomach,
forcefully squeezed. A stalwart servant
with horny hands waited upon it; I thought him
a godlike warrior, at once he grasped
heaven's tooth . . .
he blew in its eye; it barked,
its will weakened. Nevertheless it would . . .

Bellows appears to be the most likely solution because of the marked similarities between this riddle and Riddle 37, and one can set aside the solutions *cask* and *cooper* with reasonable confidence. Line 5b is missing and line 8 damaged. 'Heaven's tooth' (assuming the text is accurate in the first instance) is a striking metaphor, but its precise meaning remains uncertain; a parallel has been drawn with *As You Like It*, II, vii, 177:

> Blow, blow, thou winter wind,
> Thou art not so unkind
>   As man's ingratitude;
> Thy tooth is not so keen,
> Because thou art not seen,
>   Although thy breath be rude.

Riddle 88

[*lines 1–8 defective*]
but there I towered, where my brother and I
had grown together; we two were sturdy.
The place we lived was all the more noble
for its high ornaments. Often the wood hid us.
On dark nights the canopy of forest trees
shielded us from showers; God shaped us.
Now our kin will succeed us, mighty
as we are – younger brothers
will deprive us of our home. I am
unique on middle-earth; my back
is dark and strange. I stand on wood
at one end of the table. My brother isn't here
but, separated from him, I must stay
and stand alone at the table's end;
I don't know in which quarter or country
my brother lives as one of man's possessions,
he who once lived high beside me.
We always fought together.
We butted and rutted together; never
did either display his strength alone
or we would have both been defeated.

> Now monsters eat at my insides,
> they gouge out my guts; I cannot escape,
> He who searches will find riches in the spoor
> . . . soul's gain.

The answer is either *antler* or *inkhorn*, or both. The first eight lines are too badly damaged to reconstitute and the last line is also defective. The other (and superior) riddle relating to an antler/inkhorn is Riddle 93.

Riddle 89

Less than twenty words survive of this ten-line riddle about a creature who had a stomach. No translation is offered since they give no real idea as to the solution and embody no memorable images.

Riddle 90

This riddle is in Latin. It translates literally:

It seemed to me a wonder, the wolf is held by the lamb; / the lamb fell on to the rock and takes the bowels of the wolf. / Then might I stand and sorrow, I have seen the great glory, / two wolves standing and weeping for the third; / they have four feet, they see with seven eyes.

The meaning of these five lines, written in six-stress lines with some medial rhyme, has caused great perplexity, and no commentator has come up with a solution that has found favour with any other. Perhaps most interesting is Henry Morley's apocalyptic explanation: 'The marvel of the Lamb that overcame the wolf and tore its bowels out is of the Lamb of God who overcame the devil and destroyed his power.' He goes on to equate the 'four feet' to the four Gospels, the 'seven eyes' to the Book of Revelation and the 'two wolves' to the Old and New Testaments. Maybe, though, this is all too far-fetched. Bradley noted, 'I am strongly disposed to think it most probable that the reference is to circumstances well known to the author and to his readers, but to us quite unknown and unconjecturable'; and there, for the moment, the matter rests.

Riddle 91

Key, without the innuendo that characterizes Riddle 44. Symphosius' Riddle 4 is probably an analogue: 'I bring great power with my little strength. I open closed houses, but I close opened ones up again. I protect the home for the master, but I am protected by him in turn.'

Riddle 92

Almost five of the original seven lines survive. They read:

> I was the boast of brown ones; a tree in the forest,
> lofty life-bearer; earth's offspring;
> man's cause of joy and woman's message;
> treasure in your home. Now I'm the happy
> weapon of a warrior, with a ring . . .

The answer is widely taken to be a *beech*. The shape-changing form of this riddle, which seeks to confuse by being so many different things, is similar to Riddles 30a and 40. Frederick Tupper argues that 'the boast of brown ones' may be the beech-mast on which swine subsist; line 3, rather reminiscent of the opening of 'The Husband's Message', might refer to a rune-stave, and 'treasure in your home' could be any prized domestic object made of wood. When the Germanic tribes first came to Britain, the land lay largely under great forests of ash, oak, and beech, such as Selwood, Wychwood, Sherwood, and the Weald, which stretched from Hampshire to Kent and was 120 miles long and 30 miles wide.

Riddle 93

Ink container made from a stag's horn is accepted by all commentators except those who prefer a less specific answer, such as *horn* or *antler*. The text of lines 1–8 and lines 32–5 is defective; I have indicated the rather uneasy change from third to first person singular in line 14 by dividing that line; lines 23–4 ('I suffer pain from all those / that have bitten the shield') appear to mean that the iron weapons that have, or might have, bitten into battle-shields now hollow out the horn; the 'preying foe' in line 28 is clearly a quill that as a feather supported the raven or the eagle, which, with the wolf, were the conventional (and doubtless actual) beasts of battle. Despite the textual difficulties and Paull F. Baum's fair comment that 'the lines are ambitiously elaborate and leave the impression that the writer's reach exceeded his grasp,' the riddle contains some fresh images and is more effective than its counterpart, Riddle 88.

Riddle 94

Several critics, including the editors of *The Anglo-Saxon Poetic Records*, believe that, as with Riddles 40 and 66, the answer to this riddle is *Creation*. The text of the six lines is badly damaged but, because it contains attractive images and is strangely satisfying in its fragmentary form, a translation is offered. Postulated restorations are included in square brackets:

> [I am the] shaper . . .
> higher than heaven . . .

> . . . more brilliant than the sun,
> . . . [stronger than] steel,
> sharper than salt . . .
> loved more than all this light, brighter than [a fleece.]

Riddle 95

Riddle, *moon* and *wandering singer* have been proposed. It would be pleasant to think the poet or poets who composed the *Exeter Book* riddle collection rounded it off with a riddle about a riddle, but neither this nor the other proposals are very convincing. The poem ends:

> ic swaþe hwilum
> mine bemiþe   monna gehwylcum

'I sometimes hide my tracks from all humankind.' Because the text is evidently corrupt, those tracks are rather more blurred than the poet intended. What *wiht* or creature, animate or inanimate, can have made them? Who can say?

BIBLIOGRAPHY

Editions

Krapp, George Philip, and Dobbie, Elliot van Kirk (eds.), *The Anglo-Saxon Poetic Records* (6 vols.) (Vol. III: *The Exeter Book*), New York and London, 1931–53.

Tupper, Frederick, Jr. (ed.), *The Riddles of the Exeter Book*, Boston, 1910.

Williamson, Craig (ed.), *The Old English Riddles of the Exeter Book*, North Carolina, 1977.

Wyatt, A. J. (ed.), *Old English Riddles*, Boston, 1912.

Translations

Abbott, H. H., *The Riddles of the Exeter Book*, Cambridge, 1968.

Alexander, Michael, *Old English Riddles*, London, 1980.

Baum, Paull F., *Anglo-Saxon Riddles of the Exeter Book*, Durham, North Carolina, 1963.

Mackie, W. S. (ed. and tr.) *The Exeter Book, part 2.* London, 1934.

Williamson, Craig, *A Feast of Creatures: Anglo-Saxon Riddle-Songs.* Pennsylvania, 1982 and London, 1983.

Studies and related books

Allen, Michael J. B., and Calder, Daniel G., *Sources and Analogues of Old English Poetry*, Cambridge and New Jersey, 1976.

Greenfield, Stanley, *A Critical History of Old English Literature* ('Lore and Wisdom'), New York, 1965 and London, 1966.

Ohl, Raymond T. (ed.), *The Enigmas of Symphosius*, Philadelphia, 1928.

Taylor, Archer, *English Riddles from Oral Tradition*, Berkeley and Los Angeles, 1951.

—— *The Literary Riddle before 1600*, Berkeley and Los Angeles, 1948.